Privileged
Conversations

Privileged Conversations

DRAMATIC STORIES FOR CHRISTMAS

Richard P. Olson

UNITED CHURCH PRESS
Cleveland, Ohio

United Church Press, Cleveland, Ohio 44115
© 1996 by Richard P. Olson

Printed in the United States of America on acid-free paper

01   00   99   98   97   96   5   4   3   2   1

Library of Congress Cataloging-in-Publication Data

Olson, Richard P.
Privileged conversations : dramatic stories for Christmas /   Richard P. Olson.
p.   cm.
ISBN 0-8298-1078-1 (alk. paper)
1. Christmas stories. 2. Christmas plays. I. Title.
PN6120.95.C6047   1996
812'.54—dc20   95-51168
CIP

To the people of Prairie Baptist Church,
Prairie Village, Kansas—

They received these stories with graciousness
and enthusiasm.
They told these stories with artistry and skill.
They ad-libbed some of the best lines—
which are now included.
They are a people among whom
the Christmas miracle can happen.

Contents

Introduction

❄❄❄❄❄❄

About twenty years ago, I wanted to tell a story for the Christmas Eve service at the church I was serving. After failing to find one that fit the worship moment and the time frame, I decided to write a story myself. By the time I had imagined, composed, prepared, and told it, that story had somehow taken a hold of me. In the creating and sharing of the story, I grasped a firsthand meaning of Christmas that all too often had evaded me.

Apparently the depths of meaning that touched me affected others. As folks left the church on that crisp Wisconsin Christmas Eve, they not only thanked me for the story, but told me they looked forward to the next one. I had stretched for one, never imagining there would be another!

Nevertheless, a custom was launched that has continued every year since. Early in the fall, I sit before the Christmas scriptures and listen for some detail, some nuance, some point of departure. I look for a dialogue between my personal pilgrimage, or the church's pilgrimage, and these stories. Amazingly, I have never been disappointed. The biblical narratives have spoken to me and I have shared what I heard.

My original intent was simply spiritual enrichment for the congregation I was serving, and for me. Years later, as I appreciated other pastors' making their creative materials for Advent and Christmas available, I wondered if these stories might be of similar help. To that end, I published a collection of them entitled *The Practical Dreamer and Other Stories to Tell at Christmas* some years ago. (And while I will speak about response to that book for a moment, this current material stands on its own. It presumes no prior knowledge of the earlier volume.)

I have been thrilled with the reaction to this collection of Christmas stories. Many persons have written or spoken to me about them. I discover that these tales have had a life beyond their original purpose—to be story/sermons in worship services.

Indeed, there are at least three populations who use these materials.

One is the individual reader. Some read the stories simply for entertainment and delight. Others read them as a devotional exercise and for spiritual enrichment.

Second, the stories have been used by families, Sunday school classes, and other small groups. Several people have told me of reading them together as a family. One family took the book on their long Christmas journey to relatives and passed the travel time by reading to each other along the way. A mother reads a story to her children each morning before school for the last several days before Christmas break. Some families reread them together every Christmas.

Sunday school classes—children, youths, and adults—have read them together, as have other small groups, as an alternative lesson during Advent. Some simply read the story and let it set. Others discovered that it stirred a lively discussion and exchange of thoughts and feelings.

Third, the stories have been used for worship and other public gatherings. The stories have been found to be a useful program resource when used in Sunday morning services, Christmas Eve services, and the programs of many church and community organizations.

Some in this latter group tell me that they have experimented with doing shared storytelling or simple dramatizations of the stories. They have found these dramatizations easy to do (simply letting the characters in the stories speak for themselves) and quite effective.

As folks found innovative ways to use the stories of *The Practical Dreamer,* I too started writing my new Christmas stories in a different way—as simple narrative dramas. I did so for the same reason: to enrich the experience by enlisting the aid of other gifted storytellers. In my congregation, this practice has been wonderfully received. Even more often than before, people tell me with openness and enthusiasm that they look forward to "story Sunday." It has become a highlight during Advent each year.

And so I offer you a new set of Christmas stories out of my own life and that of the church I serve. This time they are written as play scripts. In the hope that they will continue to serve all three audiences—individuals, small groups, public gatherings—I will offer some specific helps for each at the beginning of each story. At the same time, the readers need to adapt, depending on how they intend to engage the story. I suggest that folks browse through all three of these brief sections at the beginning of each drama.

For Readings by Individuals

For individuals, I will give a beginning thought or question as a stimulus to the imagination, a prayer of openness to the story, and scripture passages to read as background or interpretation.

An individual who reads a story in dramatic form needs to do a bit of adjusting. When we read stories, we usually visualize—we create a movie or play in our minds. A drama script takes this one step further. Dramatic directions given to actors (often in parentheses) speak of emotions, motives, posture, and movement. Stage directions may be brief, but they provide important insight into character and story line.

Not all of the reader's task of imaginative visualizing is done. However, a slightly different type of ingenuity is needed to complete the transformation of drama script to story in one's mind. The individual can imagine himself or herself to be an invisible person present in conversations, dialogues, and events as the story unfolds. Dramas often provide more detailed and subtle conversations than other forms of story.

After you get past the initial awkwardness, reading play scripts is really not difficult, and it can be great fun. Give it a try. Those who previewed the scripts in this book in this way found the experience quite natural. I hope the techniques I have suggested work for you.

For Readings in Small Groups, Families, or Classes

The second audience for these stories—families, classes, groups —can enjoy the excitement of a shared experience.

The small-group leader can choose from two methods. The first is to have the story read by the group at first sight. The leader, who should already have a grasp of the story, can select readers and guide them through. The readers will see and experience the parts for the first time, as will the hearers. The second approach is to have a subgroup go through the story a time or two on its own and then read the story aloud to the larger group. This may help participants to feel more connected with the characters and the movement of the story.

If you select the first approach, be sensitive to whether the people you select are comfortable with sight reading. Some persons may have reading disabilities, and others simply may not be comfortable sight-reading aloud in front of a group. Whichever approach you select, experiencing a story with a group can be a delight.

Play readings emphasize voice and sound more than movement of the participants. The leader should be ready to do simple narration of the play setting and any movements that the hearers would need to be aware of. A very few sound effects are suggested. The leader will need to decide whether to use these or simply mention them in the narration. On the few occasions when music is used, it can be included in some simple way or mentioned by the leader.

How and where should the drama readers be arranged? In the small group, I suggest that the readers be dispersed among the group. If the group is arranged in a circle, position the readers in various parts of the circle, so that the conversation encompasses everyone rather than focuses in one place. (Of course, if the group is in a car or bus, you'll want to make the necessary adaptations.)

I will offer help on how to divide each script. Many of them have simple three- or four-member casts. For the more complicated stories, I will make suggestions for simplifying assignments.

Also, discussion questions are provided that you can use in addition to your own to propel the group into exploring and embracing the story.

For Presentations of the Play in Public

The third audience for the stories is those who present these pieces at worship and in other public gatherings.

As you prepare to present one of the stories, you will find a complete story concept but rather vague "stage directions" as to space and movement. The vagueness is necessary, for you will need to learn how to make the story work in your space.

In the church where these stories were originally told, we have an extremely small platform. We worked around communion table and pulpit, poinsettias, choir risers, and handbell stands. When the need arose, we used aisles and balcony. Your ingenuity in making this happen in your space is the beginning of the creative gift you bring to telling the stories.

The first time around, we used virtually no props and no sets. We did very simple costuming—sometimes biblical, sometimes contemporary. These gave the congregation some guidance but let them use their imaginations as well. But you don't have to approach these stories the same way we did.

Sometimes we performed the dramas as more formal play readings. We had scripts in hand, but we moved and did other actions according to stage directions. Or we did a mixed presentation, with some readers using scripts and others memorizing their parts. A number of the plays have someone sitting at a desk or table; this facilitates the use of a script if needed.

Be free in the script. Use language that feels natural and that works for each participant. The storytellers who worked with me helped get rid of some unpronounceable phrases. (We probably missed some.) Keep that process going. Some of the stories include local settings and current events. Change them to suit your needs and bring them up to date. Let them speak to you in your "now."

At times Bible passages are given in quotes and the source is cited. Variations and paraphrases are put in brackets. This is for your information. In reading the play, do not read the Bible reference information but continue in the form and style of the drama.

As you present the play, your question should be not "Did we get it right?" but "Does this story excite us? Do we feel it? Did we experience discovery as a result of our involvement in this story?" This is more likely to happen if you have first engaged the drama in individual devotion (audience one) and then read it together and processed it as a small group (audience two). If you take these steps, you have an extra benefit: you may become a short-term group with long-lasting care for one another.

These stories came to me as gifts. Through them have come additional gifts—namely the warmth and love of those *with* whom I have told these stories, and of those *to* whom I have told them. With a sense of privilege I pass them on to you. Let the telling go on. May the stories continue.

ONE

***

His Roots

For Individuals

Imagine. Imagine that the four Gospel writers gathered to discuss Jesus' roots and genealogy and that you were allowed to sit in! We might discover that the current rage over "roots" is centuries old.

While almost certainly no such conversation occurred historically, we can construct it in the vision of our minds. What follows is the way one person imagines it.

Read. Read Mark 1, Matthew 1:1–17, Luke 3:21–38, and John 1:1–18. How did each of them view Jesus' roots? What did they believe about his significance?

Pray. Loving God, in this Advent season open our eyes to Jesus—where he came from, who he was, who he is and will be for us. Renew and enrich our hearts through the sacred discoveries that lie before us. Amen.

Then *experience the story.*

For Small Groups, Families, and Classes

Plan a Group Reading of the Script. This particular play has a cast of ten persons. If this is too large for your group, all five of the women's parts could be read by one person (or shared by two), and that same person could be the chair. That would take you down to five or six reading parts.

Use the information about the persons in the play below to aid selection and to help you introduce the play and guide the participants.

Then read it through in a relaxed way. You, the coordinator, will need to fill in a bit of narration, such as the stage directions at the very end. Don't worry about goofs. Ham it up when you feel like it. Enjoy!

Discuss the Dramatic Story. Here are some possible discussion questions. Question 1 should be discussed before the play is read; questions 2–4 are for discussion after the reading.

1. Have you tried to find out about your roots, your genealogy? If so, tell a bit about it. How far back can you go? What did you discover?
2. What information did you learn about Jesus' roots and genealogy?
3. Why do you suppose Matthew included mention of the four women in his genealogy? What does this add?
4. What, if anything, does this story about genealogies add to your knowledge of Jesus? Your belief in him? How, if at all, will you view Christmas differently this year because of this experience?

For Those Presenting the Drama in Public

Building on the insights and guidance given above, here is additional information to aid in staging this drama.

Setting. The time is the present. The place is an auditorium or studio where a panel discussion might be held. Four esteemed authorities from the past are there to take part in a scholarly exploration.

About Casting and Staging

There is a panel *Chairperson* who can be either male or female. The four panelists are the Gospel writers, *Matthew, Mark, Luke,* and *John*. Perhaps you will want to have large name tags in front of them, so the audience will not forget who is speaking. It would be better to have placards or banners above them. You might want to have not only their names, but the symbols by which they have been known over the ages: the symbol for Mark is a person; for Matthew, a lion; for Luke, a calf; and for John, an eagle.

Mark should be younger than the others, abrupt, and blunt. *Matthew* should be more traditional and bookish. *Luke,* a gentle soul, is very attuned to Jesus' inclusion of all people and of women, perhaps because he is a Gentile. *John* should be portrayed as one with mystic vision to see beyond what others see.

When the play was first presented, the Gospel writers dressed in contemporary clothing. Mark wore fatigues; Matthew had a prayer shawl and yarmulke; Luke wore a lab coat; and John was dressed in white. At one point Matthew consulted his "scroll," and it was a laptop computer! These touches seemed to bring the Gospel writers closer to contemporary folks. The women appeared in biblical costume.

While no specific stage directions are given, each panelist may need to stand and possibly move about for audience interest and attention. For example, Mark might pace impatiently while responding to the chair. Matthew and Luke might stand for effect when making their concluding points, to make them stronger. John might stand throughout and see a vision far beyond the place where the panel discussion takes place.

For much of the first part of the drama, neither Luke nor John speaks, while Mark and Matthew spar a bit. Luke should look interested but somewhat puzzled at some of their concerns. John should be serene and untouched by their controversies. Other suggestions for staging are given in the text of the play.

Four women, *Tamar, Rahab, Ruth,* and *Bathsheba,* specifically mentioned in Matthew's genealogy of Jesus, each appear and speak. If you have lighting and theatrical effects, you can use them to make these characters appear and disappear. Otherwise, the women can simply come and speak when mentioned. Perhaps they can appear at center stage, with the chairperson on one side of the stage and the four panelists on the other. There is also an *Unseen Woman's Voice* that offers interpretation of some sections of Matthew's genealogy.

The Drama

CHAIRPERSON: Ever since the publication of Alex Haley's *Roots* back in 1976, people have been fascinated with their heritage. Genealogical research has become a major enterprise. Folks want to know about their ancestors. They are also eager to probe the meanings of their family trees.

Today we are going to probe the roots of Jesus of Nazareth. We are fortunate to have a uniquely qualified panel of experts to aid us in our discovery. Each has written a significant book on the subject. Will you please welcome—Mark (*He appears, looking rather disgruntled; the others look much happier to be here. As each name is called, the panelist appears, and there is applause.*) . . . Matthew . . . Luke . . . and John. (Matthew *and* Mark *should be on opposite ends of the stage so they have some room to be in opposition with each other. When* Matthew *and* Luke *come in, they carry their scrolls.*)

Welcome, and thank you for coming. Mark, let's start with you. When I called you, at first you refused to come.

MARK: That's right.

CHAIR: I wanted you so badly that I finally persuaded you to come. You made clear, however, that you came under protest. (Mark *nods, acknowledging his protest.*) If I may ask, did you not want to discuss Jesus' roots?

MARK: Because it just doesn't matter.

MATTHEW: (*rather agitated*) Mark, how could you say such a thing?

MARK: Easy, because it's true. (Matthew *becomes even more upset and begins to sputter about Mark's not getting it, when the* Chair *interrupts.*)

CHAIR: Matthew, we will give you your chance. For now, let's hear from Mark. (*speaking to Mark, picking up manuscript*) You begin your book, "The beginning of the gospel of Jesus Christ, the Son of God." Will you tell us more about your view?

MARK: There are so many significant things to tell. So I didn't bother with any genealogies or birth stories. I'll tell you what is important, if you want to know Jesus' roots. Read my book. I begin with the forerunner, John the Baptist, who speaks of how powerful Jesus will be. That's all you need to know—a voice, preparing the way for him.

MATTHEW: Mark, you ignore and miss so much!

MARK: (*ignoring Matthew*) I tell of the baptism, the temptation, his calling disciples, his healing many persons, his going to many towns—and that's just my first chapter!

CHAIR: Why do you tell the story so fast and abruptly?

MARK: Because that's who Jesus was! That's how he lived. He was a doer, an active person. He was filled with human feelings, but he was also filled with the power of God.

CHAIR: I'd like to hear more, but we must move on. Matthew, I gather you disagree.

MATTHEW: (*beginning cautiously and diplomatically*) We are all grateful to our colleague Mark for writing down many of Peter's stories of Jesus. (*changing mood and speaking strongly*) However, on this topic, his view is seriously flawed!! (Mark *and* Matthew *glare at each other.*)

CHAIR: In your view, how important is it to know Jesus' roots?

MATTHEW: Very important indeed. It tells us from whom he came and why.

CHAIR: Can you help us to know Jesus' roots?

MATTHEW: Oh yes, I researched them carefully. I will read what I discovered and wrote down. I don't want to miss a single detail!

MARK: I bet! (Matthew *grimaces, but does not let himself be distracted. He opens his scroll and begins to read, while* Mark *settles into a position of comfortable boredom.*)

MATTHEW: (*reading from his own scroll*) "The book of the genealogy of Jesus Christ, the son of David, the son of Abraham.
    "Abraham was the father of Isaac and Isaac the father of Jacob and Jacob the father of Judah and his brothers, and Judah the father of Perez and Zerah by Tamar."

MARK: (*He has been reclining and staring into space. Electrified by the mention of Tamar, he jerks up in an alert position*) Tamar? You speak of Tamar??

TAMAR: (*appears center stage*) Judah was the founder of one of the twelve tribes of Israel. He was also my father-in-law, a man who did not keep his promises to me. Er—his son, my husband—had died before we had children. Judah promised me another son that I might bear children. But he never kept his promise.
    And so, I developed a plan. When I heard my father-in-law was coming close to his sheep shearers, I put off my widow's garments. Instead I put on a veil, wrapped myself up, and sat by the entrance where he would come. He took me to be a harlot and asked my favors. I obtained from him his signet and his cord.

Later, when it was known I was pregnant, he was going to have me killed for my adultery. He would have had me burned! Then I showed them the cord and signet of the father. (*sarcastically*) Neither of us burned after that. Judah said I was more righteous than he, since he had not kept his promise. Shortly, I gave birth to twins. I did what I had to do. There was Judah's failed promises; my deception; our incest. And yet, through it all, the generations passed on to the Promised One. (*She exits or fades from view, and* Matthew *continues.*)

MATTHEW: " . . . And Perez the father of Hezron, and Hezron the father of Ram, and Ram the father of Amminadab, and Amminadab the father of Nahshon, and Nahshon the father of Salmon, and Salmon the father of Boaz by Rahab."

LUKE: Now really, Matthew, must you also speak of Rahab?

RAHAB: (*appears center stage*) Unlike Tamar, I did not simply pose as a prostitute. That *was* my livelihood, my only possible livelihood. It was an accepted way of life in my home city of Jericho, but an unpleasant, degrading one.

Then came a knock at my door that changed my life. Two strangers came to my dwelling. The officials were after them. They asked that I hide them. Somehow, almighty God told me what to do in that instant. I did indeed hide them—covered them with stalks of flax on my roof. I lied to the officials and urged them to pursue them to the Jordan. Then I let the strangers down by a rope from a window, for my house was on the city wall. Before they left, I told them that we knew the powerful God was with them, that we quaked before their coming. I knew they would conquer us. And so I asked for an oath. The oath was that my household would be spared—my father and mother and brothers and all my family. They promised and, when the conquest came, they kept their promise. In time I married. I am also a part of Jesus' family tree! (Rahab *leaves or disappears and* Matthew *continues.*)

7

MATTHEW: " . . . and Salmon the father of Boaz by Rahab, and Boaz the father of Obed by Ruth. . . ."

LUKE: I'm glad you mentioned Ruth. I agree that she belongs in this story.

RUTH: (*appears center stage*) I was an alien, a stranger, a Moabite. Usually those of Israel and of Moab stayed away from each other. However, there was a famine, and a family of Israelites sojourned among us, seeking food and work. I fell in love and married one of their sons, a man named Chilion. But our marriage was all too brief. These were harsh times, and in short order my husband, brother-in-law, and father-in-law all died.

Then Naomi, my mother-in-law, decided to return to her homeland. To be supportive, we widowed daughters-in-law offered to go with her. But she urged us to stay with our own people. My sister-in-law Orpah followed her advice and did so.

However, I was led to stay with the mother of the man I had loved and lost. I said to her, "Entreat me not to leave you or to return from following you; for where you go I will go, and where you lodge I will lodge; your people shall be my people and your God my God; where you die I will die, and there I will be buried" (Ruth 1:16–17).

And so she relented and allowed me to go with her. My offer was a hard promise to keep. She had become a bitter woman, and life with her was not easy! Our struggle for food was harsh. Often we had very little to eat. I gleaned the grain that was dropped or left in the corners of the field.

In time, Naomi's kinsman Boaz noticed me. We came to respect and love each other and were married. A son was born, and we named him Obed. When he grew to manhood, he and his wife had a son named Jesse. And though I did not live to see it, Jesse was the father of the great King David.

Israelite sacred writings said, "No . . . Moabite shall enter the assembly of the Lord, even to the tenth generation. . . ."

And yet I, an alien and stranger, was the great-grandmother of one of the greatest kings of Israel, a part of the generations that led to the Promised One.

MATTHEW: (*still reading*) "And David was the father of Solomon by the wife of Uriah."

MARK: (*amused and exasperated*) The wife of Uriah? Must you put every scandal of our people in this family tree?

BATHSHEBA: (*appears center stage*) My name is Bathsheba, and yes, I was the wife of the mighty warrior Uriah the Hittite. Once, when he was gone, King David was attracted to me and sent for me. I was flattered. He was charming, but rather old. I did not know how to say no to my king.

I thought it a harmless encounter. Then I discovered I was pregnant! After I sent word to David, events crashed about me. My husband was killed in battle. I mourned him and then came to the house of my king as wife. The child was born, but he was sickly and very shortly died.

Through all this, David loved me. In time, we had another son, Solomon. Thus I was wife of the greatest king Israel ever had and mother of its most splendid king. And I am part of Jesus' family tree. (*She exits or disappears.*)

MARK: Matthew, do you have any more scandals to throw in?

MATTHEW: No. Let's see, where was I? David was the father of Solomon.

MARK: Ah yes, the part of this history that every Hebrew child knows. Solomon, then the division of the kingdom. Generation after generation of kings. Let's see, there was Rehoboam, then Abijah, then Asa.

MATTHEW: Then Jehoshaphat, Uzziah, Jotham.

MARK: (*sing-song and bored*) Then Ahaz, Hezekiah, Manasseh. (*pauses, remembering Manasseh's wickedness, quietly*) The wicked Manasseh.

MATTHEW: Then Amos, then the great Josiah, and then Jechoniah and his brothers at the time of the deportation to Babylon.

AN UNSEEN WOMAN'S VOICE: (*perhaps one of those who spoke earlier—with gravity*) The deportation! The exile!! How the mighty have fallen. "By the waters of Babylon, there we sat down and wept, when we remembered Zion." Our cities were burned, our temple destroyed, our finest taken captive. It seemed our people were no more. And yet, we survived and waited, and hoped.

MATTHEW: (*continues reading*) "And after the deportation to Babylon: Jechoniah was the father of Shealtiel, the father of Zerubbabel, the father of Abiud." (Matthew *speaks softly as if continuing this list, pantomiming reading, while the following speech is given.*)

UNSEEN WOMAN'S VOICE: Our people were in Babylon for a few generations. Then some returned. They were allowed to build a simple temple and to rebuild the city walls. We were no longer an independent nation. Life was a constant struggle. The hope for God's Promised One, a deliverer, burned high. Surely God had brought us into being for more than we yet knew. When would the Promised One come?

MATTHEW: (*finishing the final third of the genealogy, still reading*) " . . . Matthan the father of Jacob, the father of Joseph, the husband of Mary, of whom Jesus was born, who is called the Messiah." (*pause*)

MARK: Matthew, are you *finally* finished?

MATTHEW: Yes.

MARK: Then what's your point?

MATTHEW: All the generations from Abraham to David numbered fourteen generations, and from David to the deportation to Babylon, fourteen generations, and from the deportation to Babylon to the Christ, fourteen generations.

MARK: So what?

CHAIR: (*more diplomatically*) Matthew, what does that mean to you?

MATTHEW: The whole history of the covenant people points to him. He came to fulfill what the Lord had said by the prophets.

CHAIR: What about your search for Jesus' roots?

MATTHEW: He goes back to Abraham and Sarah and to that first covenant God made with them.

LUKE: (*who has shown more interest as Matthew has been drawing his conclusions*) Matthew, you are right as far as you go. But you don't go back far enough!

MATTHEW: (*firmly, a bit defensively*) I *know* I have given a definitive account. My research was exhaustive.

MARK: (*still the cynical critic*) Exhaus*ting*!

MATTHEW: (*continuing*) What could one possibly add to my research?

CHAIR: It is time to move on to our next panelist. Luke, would you explain your criticism? What did you find in your search for Jesus' roots?

LUKE: My information is somewhat different from Matthew's at points along the way. However, that is minor. My most basic disagreement is that he doesn't go back far enough!

CHAIR: What do you mean?

LUKE: He goes back to Abraham, and the story of the Hebrew people.

MATTHEW: Of course!

LUKE: That's not far enough.

CHAIR: What do you suggest?

LUKE: I look back further, much further. May I? (Chair *nods, and* Luke *draws out his own scroll*) Matthew begins with Abraham, but I go on. (*reads*) "Abraham [was] the son of Terah, the son of Nahor . . . " (*looks up*) I look back through the ages before Abraham to Noah.

MATTHEW: The flood, the rainbow, the earlier covenant. I see what you mean.

LUKE: I speak of Methuselah.

MARK: "Methuselah lived nine hundred sixty-nine years and he died." Bor-ing!

LUKE: I go back to "Seth, the son of Adam, the son of God"!!!

CHAIR: You are saying—

LUKE: That Jesus' roots go far beyond Abraham. They go back to the origins of humankind, to the first Adam.

CHAIR: What does that mean to you?

LUKE: That Jesus is not just the fulfillment of Hebrew hopes. (Luke *excitedly rises.*) He comes from the *beginning of all creation!* My friend Paul put it well: The first Adam became a living being. The last Adam became a life-giving spirit (1 Cor. 15:45)! Jesus, the new Adam, is *a part of all people.* And he is *for all the peoples of the earth,* with mighty gifts to offer. (Luke *looks expectantly at the others. He feels that he has spoken the last word. He sits. There is silence for a moment. Then* John *gently speaks.*)

JOHN: Luke, my brother, just a moment ago, you told Matthew that his discoveries, though true, did not go far enough. Now I must tell you the same thing.

LUKE: (*humbled, but puzzled*) I do not go far enough? I don't understand. How could anyone go deeper into Jesus' roots than I have?

JOHN: You do not see far enough.

LUKE: But John, I strained my eyes to see the very beginning of creation. That is not far enough? (John *puts a caring hand on his arm and slowly shakes his head no.*) I don't understand. What more . . . (*trails off, puzzled, wondering*)

JOHN: Listen, and I will tell you. (*At this time, create a mystical, majestic atmosphere. Perhaps quiet, beautiful music from an organ. Perhaps you darken the room and project pictures of galaxies on a screen.* John *does not read from his book, but gives these words from John 1 as his own vision. He stands and sees this vision and the others see it also. Give it slow, majestically, poetically. Pause between sections.*)
"In the beginning was the Word, and the Word was with God and the Word was God. He was in the beginning with God. . . . All things were made through him. . . . "

MARK: (*more quietly than previous objections*) John, where are you? We are talking about roots.

JOHN: (*ignores him and continues*) "In the Word was life, and the life was the light of all people. . . . The light shines in the darkness and the darkness has not overcome it. . . . "

MATTHEW: John, that's beautiful, but what about roots?

JOHN: (*in his own world, seeing his own vision, continues*) "The true light that enlightens every person was coming into the world. He was in the world, and the world was made through him, yet the world knew him not. He came to his own home, and his own people received him not. But to all who received him, who believed in his name, he gave power to become the children of God. . . . (*He looks around, expecting another interruption, but there is attention and silence.*) And the Word became flesh and dwelt among us, full of grace and truth; we beheld his glory, glory as of the only Son from the Father. . . . And from his fullness have we all received grace upon grace."

LUKE: John, you speak truth. I still don't know what you want to say about Jesus' roots.

JOHN: Don't you see, Luke? Finally, you cannot trace Jesus' roots, for they proceed from the creative love of the Godhead itself! (*There is a pause for a few moments.*)

CHAIR: I'm afraid you lost us, John.

MARK: (*quietly, not as sarcastic*) He often does!

CHAIR: I need interpretation.

JOHN: My brothers have searched for Jesus' *human* roots and have debated going back to Abraham or Adam. I look *beyond* and see Jesus as coming from the very heart of God!

CHAIR: (*Puzzled and in too deep. Looks at watch or clock on wall. Has a happy thought how to bring this to a close.*) I'm afraid our time is almost gone. To conclude, I'd like to ask each panelist for a closing statement. In your search for Jesus' roots, what have you concluded?

MARK: Jesus is very God, very man who suddenly comes among us, doing many things. He heals our wounds, calls us to service, and brings us salvation.

MATTHEW: Jesus is the fulfillment of prophecy, the one for whom generations of covenant people waited.

LUKE: Jesus comes from the foundation of creation, from Adam and Eve, and is available for every person of every nation in every age, in all the earth.

JOHN: Jesus is the Word and truth that existed in God from the beginning. He is the light and grace that proceeds from God to your heart and mine.

CHAIR: We have had a most (*gulps*) stimulating discussion. Thank you and good day.

MARK: (*stands and walks over to the Chair*) Just a minute. This isn't just information you hear and forget. (*The others follow him.*) This is a story that calls for a response.

MATTHEW: It is evidence that demands a verdict.

LUKE: We have told you what we believe. Now we want to know how you respond to the one who is . . . friend to all.

(*Each of the others chimes in spontaneously.*)

MATTHEW: The Promised One.

MARK: Our Savior and deliverer.

JOHN: The Light of the World. He is—
(*Recorded music or choir bursts into the refrain from the "Hallelujah Chorus"*): "King of kings and Lord of lords. And he shall reign forever and ever. King of kings, and Lord of lords. Forever and ever. Amen."
(*The four stand around Chair with various expressions of prayer and praise, but very aware that Chair is still seated. At the climax of the music Chair tentatively rises, sees the smiles and encouragement of the others, and begins to smile with delight, holding arms in a receiving position. As the music ends,* John *speaks.*)

JOHN: (*lovingly*) I'm glad you see what we see and respond as we do! (*The others greet enthusiastically, and chatting happily away, they walk off the stage, arms on Chair's shoulder, or with other expressions of welcome and support.*)

TWO

❋❋❋❋❋

The Other Birth Story

For Individuals

Imagine. Imagine simple people in a humble village in a long-ago time. These are folks who struggle to believe in a God of promise even when there is very little outward evidence to cause them to do so.

Read. Read Luke 1:5–25, 39–45, 57–80.

Pray. God, how could you have used such people as Zechariah and Elizabeth so powerfully? Do you have more surprises for us? Is there some way you can use me? If so, I am your humble servant. In Jesus' name. Amen.

Then *experience the story.*

For Small Groups, Families, and Classes

Plan a Group Reading of the Script. While this script includes a number of persons, there are just three who participate throughout: Luke the narrator (who could do the additional narrating), Zechariah, and Elizabeth. Two or three other persons could read multiple parts and fill in as the persons with whom they interact in the succeeding episodes.

For fun, you might want to write out the "one-liners" from neighbors at the birth scene and hand them to folks who don't have a larger part. You might prepare the whole group to be neighbors at that scene. They should be ready to cheer and dance if a baby is born!

There are two points in the play where, for those performing the script, pantomime is indicated. The first—Zechariah's encounter in the temple—is narrated by Zechariah and can be done simply in that fashion. In the second, the now mute Zechariah communicates to Elizabeth what has happened and what is promised. You need to anticipate, and either narrate or have Zechariah and Elizabeth ready to pantomime that scene.

Discuss the Dramatic Story. Here are some possible discussion questions. Question 1 should be discussed before the play has been read; questions 2–4 are to be used after the reading.

1. Have the group divide into subgroups of three or so persons. Then suggest these questions for sharing: What stories are told about your birth? What was your birth order? Where were you born? Do you know any other details? How does your birth story help you know who you are?
2. At what points in the story did you feel closest to Zechariah? To Elizabeth? Why do you suppose God used them for this important task?
3. What feelings or attitudes did this story stir in you?
4. In what way does this Bible story contribute to the biblical teaching about hope?

For Those Presenting the Drama in Public

Setting. A village in Judea, a long time ago.

Cast of Characters

LUKE: A compassionate storyteller, author of the Gospel from which this story is taken.

ZECHARIAH: An elderly man who has lived a hard life with many disappointments. He has survived because of a twinkle in his eye and a self-deprecating sense of humor, which express a persistent but undramatic faith. Zechariah somewhat resembles Tevye in *Fiddler on the Roof.*

ELIZABETH: An elderly woman and the wife of Zechariah. She too has had many disappointments—most notably childlessness. This has hit her harder, and she correspondingly lacks Zechariah's twinkle. In the opening scene she is a depressed, despondent person who has given up on life. As the story progresses her zest returns.

Other characters are needed to aid in telling the story of these two people. They include: WOMAN FROM THE AUDIENCE (one or two persons); JOEL, a fellow priest; NAHUM, Joel's twelve-year-old son; HIGH PRIEST; TOWNSPEOPLE; TWO NEIGHBORS; and a MIDWIFE.

To the Actors and Storytellers. This is an attempt to use story and drama to bring to life a rather difficult and often ignored part of scripture. This Bible passage is part of the account of the preparation for the coming of Jesus.

The drama is an attempt to communicate two truths: the touch of the divine on ordinary human beings like us, and the usefulness to the divine of ordinary human beings like us. These truths will be experienced if the witnesses of the drama sense their closeness to and similarity to the two central characters, Zechariah and Elizabeth. Since this is a brief drama, with little time for character development, those who play these characters must feel deeply into the parts, become these persons, and send out those signals that call forth identification with them all at once.

The Form. This is a mixed form, using storytelling, dramatic scenes, and interaction with the congregation (over the centuries!). It has a number of settings. When first presented, the play was performed with simple costumes and virtually no scenery or props. Various parts of the sanctuary—center aisle, space on floor in front of pulpit, pulpit area, choir loft—were used for the different settings and events.

The Drama

(*At the beginning, only Luke is onstage, sitting at a writing desk at one side of the playing area.*)

LUKE: (*quill pen in hand, writing on scroll and reading aloud what he has written*) "Inasmuch as many have undertaken to compile a narrative of the things which have been accomplished among us, just as they were delivered to us by those who from the beginning were eyewitnesses and ministers of the Word, it seemed good to me, having followed all these things closely for some time past, to write an orderly account for you, most excellent Theophilus (*looks straight at congregation on this word—assume that the congregation is Theophilus, literally "God lover"*), that you may know the truth of the things of which you have been informed (Luke 1:1–4). (*Becomes rather intense at this point. Then relaxes, pauses, begins to see the story he is telling and relates it in a more conversational tone.*)

"In the days of Herod, King of Judea, there was a priest named Zechariah (Zechariah *appears*) of the division of Abijah; and he had a wife of the daughters of Aaron, and her name was Elizabeth. And they were both righteous before God, walking in all the commandments and ordinances of God blameless" (Luke 1:5–6).

(Zechariah *listens to this description with mild amusement and a slight chuckle now and then.*)

ZECHARIAH: When Luke says we were righteous and blameless, he really meant we were ordinary! Dull!! (*chuckles again*) Oh, we tried to be fair in all our dealings and faithful in our prayers. But don't many do that? Nothing unusual about us.

I feel awkward talking to you, a stranger. You ask, Shouldn't a priest have more social graces? (*laughs*) I'm not a priest, not by profession. I'm a poor struggling farmer. I have a few olive trees, a little land.

You see, I'm simply a priest by heritage. I am a descendant of the great Aaron, brother of Moses. (*grins*) But Aaron has lots of descendants (*chuckles*) and his tribe increases all the time. As near as I can figure there must be nearly twenty-five thousand of us. And so for generations we have been divided into twenty-four divisions. I am in the eighth division, of Abijah. Twice a year we go to be the priests at the temple for seven days. Even then there are about a thousand of us. I am not needed, not really. Never once in all the years that I have gone have I been chosen to burn the incense and give the blessing on the people.

You ask then, why do I go? For the pay? That's a laugh! We give our time and pay our own expenses. (*becomes more quiet, revealing a deeper part of himself than before*) I go because for that one week I am somebody. I'm no longer a poor farmer going nowhere. The blood of Aaron flows in my veins. The mighty God who delivered Moses and Aaron is my God. I am in the company of those who serve the God of Abraham, of Isaac, of Jacob. (*very personal*) In ways I can't tell you, I gain the hope to keep on from those days as a priest in Jerusalem. (*Stares intently at the imaginary person before him with whom he has been visiting, then suddenly turns away, a bit embarrassed at revealing his deeper self. He turns and calls*).

ZECHARIAH: Elizabeth. Elizabeth.

(Elizabeth *appears. She has a flat affect and seems dull and depressed.*)

ELIZABETH: (*looking away and down*) Yes, Zechariah.

ZECHARIAH: It is time I leave for my duties in the temple.

ELIZABETH: (*tonelessly, without feeling*) Yes, I know. Go in peace.

ZECHARIAH: Will you be all right? (*He waits for an answer, but there is none. He goes on, struggling for some conversation, some contact between them before he leaves.*) It is the fallow season, so the fields need no attention. But if there is any problem, call for Nathan. He will help, as I will help during his week next month. (*Still no comment. Zechariah struggles to say something, so that they will feel some bond between them before he goes.*) Nathan said his children will look in on you each evening to be sure you are safe. (*This was the wrong thing to say. She shudders when he says it and then responds with a sob.*)

ELIZABETH: A helpless old woman cared for by her *neighbor's* children. How I wish I had *my own* children to care for me.

ZECHARIAH: Elizabeth, please. (*She rather quickly stops sobbing, not being the type to allow herself many tears. Zechariah reaches out and touches her arm. Though they have been married for many years, he has not forgotten how to be tender.*) Daughter of Aaron? (Elizabeth *smiles just a bit.*)

ELIZABETH: I know you must be on your way, son of Aaron. (*gives him a perfunctory kiss on the cheek*) It's just that when you are away, it hits me how empty my arms are, how lonely I really am. No child, no fulfillment, no promise.

ZECHARIAH: (*eager to escape this circular conversation that has gone on for years*) I will return as quickly as I can. Shalom? (*a question with a touch of hope*)

ELIZABETH: (*without enthusiasm*) Shalom. (*They drop arms. Zechariah walks a few steps and then turns his back to the audience, standing still.*)

LUKE: "But they had no child, because Elizabeth was barren, and both were advanced in years."

WOMAN FROM AUDIENCE: (*speaks with compassion, but just a little bit of condescension, to Elizabeth, not satisfied with Elizabeth's attitude*) Elizabeth, not having a child is not the end of the world!

ELIZABETH: For me it was.

WOMAN FROM AUDIENCE: Jesus said that you didn't have to bear and suckle children to be blessed. You could find blessing in believing and serving.

ELIZABETH: You know that, I didn't.

WOMAN FROM AUDIENCE: There are many ways to be fulfilled as a woman.

ELIZABETH: For me there was only one. (*with tragic finality*) And it was closed to me. Forever. I wish I could make you understand how dead I felt inside. (*holds a moment and then exits*)

ZECHARIAH: I did not have the same joy as usual as I left for Jerusalem this time. I have always been a person of hope—worshiping our great God gives me hope! But sometimes the lamp of my hope burns low. It was burning very low that morning.
    I did not feel the usual excitement in greeting my friends on the way. (*Greets imaginary fellow travelers, smiling and with warmth. A sadness returns to his face after the greeting.*) "Hello, Lamech. . . . Good journey to you, Joda. . . . May you have joy in serving God, Neeri."

JOEL: (*calling from a distance with enthusiasm*) Zechariah, Zechariah! (*Runs up to him. They are old friends and embrace warmly.*) May you find joy in serving God.

ZECHARIAH: And may you, old friend.

JOEL: May the lot fall on you to burn the incense and give the blessing.

ZECHARIAH: I pray the blessing be yours.

JOEL: I want you to meet someone. Nahum! (*His twelve-year-old son runs up to him. Joel is just bursting with pride.*) This is my son! His first time as a member of the brotherhood of priests. The sons of Aaron will continue to future generations! (Zechariah *greets Nahum with a dignified handshake and words of welcome.* Joel *grabs Nahum by the hand, like a little boy.*) Come on, son! Let's be on our way.

NAHUM: (*pulls hand away*) Father! I'm a man, remember?

JOEL: (*laughing*) Oh yes, yesterday a boy, today a man. Come along, my man. (*His arm lightly on Nahum's shoulder, they walk off jauntily.* Zechariah *sadly watches.*)

ZECHARIAH: Elizabeth's sadness was my sadness too, but I could not speak of it, even admit it, or she would have felt even worse. How I envied Joel and his son Nahum that day. How I would have given anything to exchange places with him. But I guessed it was not to be.

I had never asked God for much, but even my few simple requests seemed to be denied.

Maybe that's what trust in God really is—to keep on hoping when there's no evidence to help you hope. I keep on trusting when no reason is seen to go on. I hope God honors my simple trust. (*He slowly walks to the front of the sanctuary.*)

LUKE: "Now while he was serving as priest before God when his division was on duty according to the custom of the priesthood, it fell to him by lot to enter the temple of the Lord and burn incense."

(*While Luke speaks, the following is pantomimed. The* High Priest *offers an imaginary bag filled with rocks to several imaginary priests, and to Joel, Nahum, and Zechariah.* Zechariah *looks with wonder at his rock—it probably was white, or had a word inscribed on it. Still gazing at his rock with wonder and reverence, he approaches the High Priest.*)

ZECHARIAH: (*holds out the rock—humbly and with great awe*) God has chosen me!

HIGH PRIEST: Do you know what to do?

ZECHARIAH: I think so.

HIGH PRIEST: Enter the court of the priests, and burn this incense upon the altar within. As you do so, offer your prayers on behalf of the people of Israel. When you are finished, come back to this rail and offer a blessing upon the worshipers. Do you understand? (Zechariah *nods, still in an awed daze. The* High Priest *signals and* Joel *and* Nahum *come with priestly robe and incense pot for him. With great reverence, he slowly walks to make the offering as others assume a position of silent prayer.*)

(*This next section—Zechariah's memory and the dialogue with Gabriel—is prerecorded. A tape recording of this narration is played while Zechariah pantomimes these motions.*)

ZECHARIAH: My heart was in my throat as I approached the court of the priests, a room I had never entered before. To be chosen, to speak before God of my people's needs, filled my heart with fright and awe.

I put the incense in place, and lighted it as I had been instructed.

Then I knelt in prayer. "O gracious Holy One, God of Abraham, of Isaac, of Jacob, deliverer of Moses, hear our cry. Be with your poor and long-suffering people. Give us confidence in your might and power. Give us strength to endure these difficult and bitter days. Make us a people of hope once again. (*a short pause*)

"And, uh, uh, if you could nudge my wife Elizabeth so she would be a little less bitter and sad, I'd appreciate that, too. Thine is the glory. Amen."

I looked up from my prayer, and the place was filled with a strange and blinding light!! What was that I saw on the right side of the altar of incense. Was it a person? No, it could not be. No one else was allowed there! My imagination? An angel??? I was terrified, but then I heard a voice.

GABRIEL: "Do not be afraid, Zechariah, for your prayer is heard, and your wife Elizabeth will bear you a son, and you shall call his name John."

ZECHARIAH: Too stunned to speak, I listened as he went on.

GABRIEL:

> And you will have joy and gladness,
> and many will rejoice at his birth;
> for he will be great before God,
> and he shall drink no wine or strong drink,
> and he will be filled with the Holy Spirit
> even from his mother's womb.
> And he will turn many of the sons of Israel to God,
> and he will go before him in the spirit and power of Elijah,
> to turn the hearts of the parents to the children
> and the disobedient to the wisdom of the just,
> to make ready for God a people prepared. (Luke 1:14–17)

ZECHARIAH: I couldn't believe it. All my life I had longed for a sense of the Holy One in my life. Now here was a messenger telling me we would have a child who would be a mighty spokesman for God. It was too much, and I blurted out, "How shall I know this? For I am an old man and my wife is advanced in years!" I was answered—

GABRIEL: "I am Gabriel, who stand in the presence of God; and I was sent to speak to you and to bring you this good news. And behold, you will be silent and unable to speak until the day that these things come to pass, because you did not believe my words, which will be fulfilled in their time!"

ZECHARIAH: And then it was over. I paused, deeply shaken, not sure whether what happened was true or not. I pulled myself together and prepared to go out and give the blessing.

(*end of recorded part*)

(Joel, Nahum, *and the* High Priest *have been standing silently in an attitude of prayer throughout this scene.*)

JOEL: (*to High Priest*) It has been such a long time, do you suppose some evil has befallen him?

HIGH PRIEST: I do not know.

JOEL: Don't you think you should send someone to his aid?

HIGH PRIEST: We will wait a little longer. Look, he comes to give the blessing now.

(Zechariah *appears, his face not frightened as when he entered the court of the priests, but now reflecting some "holy secret." He exchanges glances with Joel, who is bewildered by his look.* Zechariah *slowly walks to the place where he is to give the blessing. He raises his arms and tries to speak, but only air escapes from his lips. This has a strong and immediate impact on all present.* Zechariah *views this inconvenience with delight: he had forgotten what Gabriel had said about being unable to speak, but for him it confirms the vision. The others onstage are horrified at what has happened to him.*)

NAHUM: (*very frightened*) He cannot speak!

HIGH PRIEST: Something terrible has happened to him. The burden of holy duties was too great.

JOEL: No, perhaps something wonderful has happened to him. Maybe he saw a beautiful vision. In God's own time, he will make it known to us.

(Zechariah, *touched by this insight, reaches out to Joel in a firm handshake/embrace of spiritual kinship. This scene— Nahum and the High Priest horrified, Joel and Zechariah sharing a spiritual secret—holds for a pause and through Luke's next brief speech. Then they proceed as directed.*)

LUKE: And when the time of service was ended, he went to his own home.

(Zechariah, Joel, *and* Nahum *walk down the "road"—center aisle— together about halfway and then bid each other a wordless farewell.* Zechariah *turns down the aisle walking home. He starts slowly, then runs ever more swiftly, as fast as an old man can run—short steps, a bit uncertain on feet when he tries to rush, quite out of breath. He comes up to* Elizabeth, *who is seated onstage, still depressed.*)

ELIZABETH: (*looks up as* Zechariah *touches her on the shoulder, then looks down again*) Hello, son of Aaron. Did you have a safe journey? Were your friends able to go with you? (*She becomes aware that something is amiss.*) Zechariah, what's wrong? Speak to me!!

(*Then begins a pantomime. With gestures,* Zechariah *explains the vision.* Elizabeth *is puzzled. He pantomimes that the vision*

*was that they would have a baby. He takes her open, empty
arms and folds them as if to cradle a child. Elizabeth is first
upset, then unbelieving, then curious, then amused, then down-
right joyful. In this pantomime, she is transformed. She becomes alive, animated, looking people straight in the eye. She
remains so throughout the rest of the play. At the end of this
pantomime, their hands are intertwined as if together holding
their as yet imaginary child-to-be. After holding for a moment,*
Zechariah *leaves the stage.*)

LUKE: After these days, his wife Elizabeth conceived. And for
five months, she hid herself, saying—

ELIZABETH: (*joyously*) Thus God has done to me in the days
when God looked on me to take away my reproach.

Some days I think Zechariah is still bewildered by *his* vision. But *my* vision grows more certain every day. This life,
this promise I carry within me, is a wondrous gift indeed.
Someday I hope Zechariah can speak and tell me all that the
vision said about this child of ours. For now I am content. Any
child is a special gift from God. But this promised child, this
vision child, this gift-from-God child will do great things, I am
sure!

In my sixth month, my younger kinswoman Mary came to
visit me. The child in my womb leaped to greet the child within
hers! The joy, the ecstasy we felt! Oh, the harmony we enjoyed
in our shared hope!

Before these events, I must confess I felt the Almighty had
punished, or at least forgotten me. Now we are drawn up on the
whole act of divine deliverance. Somehow we knew that God
was going to use our children in the redemption of Israel.

It was so good to have someone with whom I could share
these secrets. We enjoyed each other so much that Mary stayed
longer than she intended—nearly three months. When my time
was near, she returned to Nazareth to face rather difficult family matters there.

And I grew ever more eager for that day when finally I would see my child, the gift of God. (*She turns and exits.*)

LUKE: The time grew near.

(*Townspeople and neighbors gather,* Joel *and* Nahum *among them.*)

LUKE: Now the time came for Elizabeth to be delivered.

NEIGHBOR ONE: I hear she went into labor. Did you hear anything?

NEIGHBOR TWO: No, but let's wait around for a while. Perhaps there will be news soon. Shh—here comes the midwife now. (*There is an air of expectancy.*)

MIDWIFE: Good news! Elizabeth has delivered. (*the crowd cheers*) Mother and child are fine. (*More cheers.* Midwife *goes out and escorts Elizabeth to a chair.*) Here she is! (*There are cheers again.* Midwife *is enjoying the curiosity about the child and plays it up a bit. She comes out once more with a swaddled doll in her arms.*) And here is their *son!* (*More cheers, music, a spontaneous, brief folk dance.* Elizabeth *looks on, beaming and holding the child. The dance ends and* Luke *speaks.*)

LUKE: Her neighbors and kinsfolk heard that God had shown great mercy to her, and they rejoiced with her.

MIDWIFE: (*to Elizabeth*) I suppose you will name him Zechariah after his father?

ELIZABETH: (*looking at her child*) Not so. He shall be called John.

NEIGHBOR ONE: None of your relatives are called by that name.

NEIGHBOR TWO: The father should have something to say about this. What do you think, Zechariah? (*He gestures for something to write on.*) He wants a tablet (*Someone hands him one.*)

MIDWIFE, NEIGHBORS ONE AND TWO: (*looking over his shoulder and reading one word at a time*) His . . . name . . . is . . . John!

MIDWIFE: I still don't understand. Why John?

ZECHARIAH: (*speaks clearly*) Because the vision commanded it! (*There is a sense of excitement, people say, "He speaks," "His voice is back," etc. Then silence as* Zechariah *continues.*) Because "John" means "God's gift." God *is* gracious. How I praise God for giving us this child!

(*There is a sense of wonder that grows as people look on for Luke's and Zechariah's next speech.*)

LUKE: And they all marveled. . . . And fear came on all their neighbors and kinsfolk. All these things were talked about through all the hill country of Judea; and all who heard laid them up in their hearts, saying, "What then will this child be?" For the hand of God was with him.

And his father Zechariah was filled with the Holy Spirit and prophesied, saying—

ZECHARIAH:

> Blessed be the God of Israel,
> for God has visited and redeemed God's people
> and has raised up a horn of salvation for us
> in the house of God's servant David.
> As God spoke by the mouth of the holy prophets from
> of old
> that we should be saved from our enemies
> and from the hand of all who hate us

to perform the mercy promised to our ancestors
and to remember God's holy covenant.
(*goes to Elizabeth, takes the child and holds the child up*)
And you, child, will be called prophet of the most high;
for you will go before the Lord to prepare his ways
to give knowledge of salvation to his people
in the forgiveness of their sins
through the tender mercy of our God
when the day shall dawn upon us from on high
to give light to those who sit in the shadow of death,
to guide our feet into the way of peace. (Luke 1:68–72,
76–79)

(*With a sense of climax and finality, peace and accomplishment, he hands the child back to Elizabeth. They gaze with love and joy at each other and the child for a moment. Then* Zechariah *turns and moves a few steps away. The story has a transition here. Zechariah has told their story and is finished. However, the hearers are not!*)

ZECHARIAH: Well, that's our story.

VOICE FROM THE AUDIENCE: (*can be the woman who spoke to Elizabeth, or someone else*) Wait a minute. You're not finished yet. Stories don't end with babies being born! What became of the child?

ZECHARIAH: I don't know. We had to trust the Almighty for that. Elizabeth and I died before he grew to manhood.

LUKE: I can tell you. The child grew and became strong in spirit, and he was in the wilderness till the day of his manifestation to Israel. In his manhood, he preached in the wilderness. He proclaimed a baptism of repentance for the forgiveness of sins. He was what the angel said he would be: the one to prepare the way of the Lord.

VOICE FROM THE AUDIENCE: Oh. (*half-satisfied, still puzzled by the story*) Zechariah, I must admit I don't understand you. All my life I've longed for some certainty, some sign that my faith is true. You had that vision, that sign, and you didn't believe it!

ZECHARIAH: (*with a shrug and a chuckle*) I know. As you people would say, I blew it! I've often pondered that. I too wanted certainty of God's presence and direction. When it came to me so vividly, I backed away and doubted.

VOICE FROM THE AUDIENCE: Why did you do that?

ZECHARIAH: I think I now know why. The news was so good I couldn't believe it. Maybe that's why you people these days have a hard time believing in Jesus, the one who came to us. The news of him is so good that you have a hard time believing it as well.

VOICE FROM THE AUDIENCE: I'll think about that. I have one more question. When I read the Bible, I think of the people I meet there as strong and powerful, as heroic. You folks were so ordinary.

ELIZABETH: We were nobodies.

VOICE FROM THE AUDIENCE: I'm sorry, I didn't mean to—

ELIZABETH: That's quite all right. You are right. We were unknown people, weak and fallible like anyone else. I had even quit believing or hoping. Zechariah couldn't believe the angel. But the Almighty used us—frail as we were. And we became part of God's acts to bring redemption to the whole world.

Perhaps that's the best part of our story—not that God used us, but that God can use you. (*This last line is said hesitantly, as if she is thinking out loud.*)

JOEL: As Jesus once said, "I thank you, God, that you have hidden these things from the wise and understanding, and revealed them to babes."

LUKE: Or as one of my friends put it, "God chose what is foolish in the world to shame the wise; God chose what is weak in the world to shame the strong."

ELIZABETH: (*with growing assurance and forcefulness*) Yes, I see it clearly now. God's presence and guidance are available to all. The most important part of our story is not that God used *us,* but that God can use *you!*

ZECHARIAH: And you.

(*echoing, getting softer*)

JOEL: And you.

NAHUM: And you.

(*Everyone in cast looks at audience intently, expectantly, looking for the gifts to come. This should be held for a slow count of five.*)

LUKE: Amen.

(*Then, led by Zechariah and Elizabeth carrying their child, the cast joyfully processes down the middle aisle before the closing hymn is announced.*)

❋❋❋❋❋

THREE

A Talk with an Unwanted Guest: Perspectives from the Apostle Paul

For Individuals

Imagine. Have you ever wished that there was some great person in history whom you could interview? If so who would that person be?

In this story, there is opportunity to interview the apostle Paul (in our imaginations, of course). If you could have been one of the panelists, what would you have asked?

Read. Read Galatians 4:4–6 and Philippians 2:5–11.

Pray. Majestic Creator, how you have stretched the minds of the most wise! How many are the ways that folks have understood the coming of Christ. Open my heart and mind that I may see, believe, and grasp with my heart more of what the Promised One means to me. Amen.

Then *experience the story.*

For Small Groups, Families, and Classes

Plan a Group Reading of the Script. This drama has a small, simple cast, just four persons. If you need to reduce your reading cast by one more, a single person could read the parts of Panelist Two and the Director.

Discuss the Dramatic Story. Here are some possible discussion questions. Question 1 can be discussed before the play is read; questions 2–5 are for use after the reading.

1. Have you ever come to appreciate someone you previously disliked? Or perhaps someone you vigorously disagreed with? If so, would you tell the others about this experience?
2. How did you feel about Panelist Two's attitude toward Paul? Have you ever felt this same way about the Paul we find in the scriptures? Why or why not?
3. Why do you imagine Paul ignored and/or evaded questions about Christ's birth early in the interview?
4. When Paul did get around to speaking of his views on Christ's birth, what did he actually say? How does this enrich our understanding of Christ's birth? (You may want to have the person playing Paul reread those parts bit by bit and invite the group to discuss each part after it is read.)
5. What would you like to take from this to guide you in your thinking and believing about Christmas?

For Those Presenting the Drama in Public

In addition to the guidance already offered, here is information to aid in staging this drama.

Setting. The present. A television studio where a nationally syndicated news-and-opinion interview show is taped.

Cast of Characters. The play can be performed by four persons.

PANELIST ONE: Host of a national news interview show, a reconciler of opposing viewpoints.

PANELIST TWO: A guest journalist on the show, driving, sarcastic, cynical. (*When this play was originally pre-*

sented, Panelist One was male, Panelist Two female. Persons of either gender can portray the panelists and the Director.)

DIRECTOR: An unseen voice from the balcony, giving direction and order to an otherwise chaotic program.

THE APOSTLE PAUL: Wordy, opinionated, not a good listener, but filled with power when he speaks of Christ. (*The person portraying Paul should not cite the scripture references given within this script. They are given to help the actor in preparation.*)

Form. Using a familiar talk-show format, the storytellers seek a new perspective on the Christmas story. A stretch of imagination is required to talk with a guest from hundreds of years ago. Through the clash of cultures, temperaments, personalities, one person's perspective is made clear.

[Note: A very simple staging is anticipated. The two panelists, in contemporary dress, sit at a table. The Director will be unseen throughout and will be presumed to be speaking from the balcony. Paul will be in biblical costume. There is a stool for him to sit on, though he rarely uses it. Everyone but Paul, therefore, may have a script in front of them. Though reference is made to cameras and studio paraphernalia, those may all be imaginary props.]

The Drama

PANELIST ONE: (*to Panelist Two as she or he arrives*) Am I glad to see you! I was afraid that the Christmas edition of *Face the World* might have to be canceled. Thanks for filling in!

PANELIST TWO: Glad to. Who are we interviewing for this Christmas special? Mary of Nazareth?

PANELIST ONE: No. The other network beat us to her.

PANELIST TWO: Joseph?

PANELIST ONE: (*shaking head*) He refused. Too shy. Said he wouldn't know what to say.

PANELIST TWO: Luke? Matthew?

PANELIST ONE: They were both out on assignment. Neither could come.

PANELIST TWO: Who is our guest then? (Panelist One *shows a card with a name on it.* Panelist Two *grimaces in disgust.*) Oh no! Not *him!* What does *he* know about all this?

PANELIST ONE: It will be our job to find out.

PANELIST TWO: I'll bet he knows nothing at all. But that won't keep the old windbag from going on forever. Did you hear about Eutychus over in Troas?

PANELIST ONE: No.

PANELIST TWO: This teenager was at a gathering where our *esteemed* guest spoke. He talked so long that Eutychus sank into a deep sleep. Still the old goat talked on. Eutychus fell out of an upstairs window, where he was sitting. What did that senile old geezer do? Go down, wake that teenager up, heal him. Then take him up to listen to him some more! How long is this show? Five or six hours?

PANELIST ONE: Thirty minutes, as you well know.

PANELIST TWO: We'd better be on our toes or your ratings will go to sleep before he finishes his ramble.

DIRECTOR: (*interrupting, a voice that is heard but not seen*) Silence on the set! Places everyone. (*a few moments of silence*) Okay, roll it!

PANELIST ONE: (Panelist Two, *"off camera," grimaces as* Panelist One *gives this flowery introduction.*) Good day and welcome to a special Christmas edition of *Face the World.* Today we have a most distinguished guest—the world-famous author, traveler, church planter, and evangelist—

DIRECTOR: (*interrupting*) Cut! Where is your guest? Green room, wake up and get him out here!

(Paul *appears, looking a bit confused and disoriented.*)

PAUL: Hello. I was just talking to the persons cleaning the hall out there. They hadn't heard the story!

PANELIST ONE: (*gestures to Paul to take his seat, then speaks to Director*) Hold on a minute. I need to clear up one thing. (*to Paul*) I am not clear—I have two names here. Is it Saul or Paul?

PAUL: Both are correct. "Saul" is my Jewish name. It speaks of my glorious Hebrew heritage—the tribe of Benjamin, circumcised on the eighth day, a lover of God's Word. "Paul" is my Greek name. It signifies that Christ Jesus has made me ambassador to the world. Call me Paul.

DIRECTOR: This is all very nice, but our schedule is already a shambles. Can we get on with this taping? Pick up the end of the introduction.

PANELIST ONE: . . . the famous traveler, author, church planter, and evangelist, Paul—ambassador to the world. Welcome, Mr. Paul!

PAUL: (*Immediately goes into a very "preachy" style. During this speech,* Panelist One *looks chagrined, and* Panelist Two *looks quite disgusted.*) I count it all privilege in any time or place to preach the unsearchable riches of the One who called us out of the shadows to marvelous light. My speech is simple and plain, but it is filled with the spirit and the power of the One who called me. For I am not ashamed of the gospel. It is the power of God unto salvation for all who believe, Jew, Roman, and Greek alike.

DIRECTOR: (*shouting*) CUT!! (*loud, and with authority*) Paul, Paul, why are you doing this to me?

PAUL: (*awestruck, looking up*) Lord?

DIRECTOR: No, not the Lord. I am the director.

PAUL: Director?

DIRECTOR: The leader of this show. You are not following our directions.

PAUL: I'm sorry. That's what my other leader tells me sometimes. What do you want me to do?

DIRECTOR: For one thing, don't bounce all over the place. Sit down. Don't preach, just talk in a nice quiet voice.

PAUL: I will try to do that.

DIRECTOR: A couple things more. Answer their questions. And, if you must move around a little, stay in the camera range. See those lines on the floor? They're your marks. Stay within them.

PAUL: Oh yes, I see them now. This space looks to be about the size of a prison cell I once lived in, for many months. I just

40

didn't see the walls or the bars this time. I think I can live within your marks, Mr. Leader. I will try to be your obedient servant.

DIRECTOR: Good. Now let's get going. Panel, proceed with your questions.

PANELIST TWO: Paul, did you not know the Christmas story?

PAUL: Christmas?

PANELIST ONE: You know, the birth of Jesus in Bethlehem.

PAUL: Oh, that. Yes, I knew it. Luke was my good friend. He loved those baby stories. Talked to everyone he met who might be able to tell him a little more. He repeated them so many times that I knew them as well as he did.

PANELIST TWO: Then why did you never speak about Christmas, about the birth of Jesus?

PAUL: (*thinking out loud, speaking to himself*) Christ mass. Christ-mass. Christ worship. Worship of the Christ born among us. (*then speaking out loud, directly to two*) I did speak about the birth of Jesus.

PANELIST TWO: (*momentarily confused*) Really? I don't seem to recall—

PAUL: (*interrupting*) Let me tell you about the birth of Jesus. (*Relives the following story in telling it. It is told with power and conviction—the central truth about him.*)
   I was a proud but unhappy man. Others said I was so promising and so zealous. That gave me no joy. I knew what I was like inside—a pile of filthy rags that could not make themselves clean. How I longed to be pure, righteous, and happy.

Those "Followers of the Way" had such simple joy that they nearly drove me insane! I joined in persecuting them all the way to Damascus—may God forgive me.

On the way to Damascus a dazzling light burst upon me, casting me to the ground. A voice spoke, "Saul, Saul, why are you persecuting me?"

"Who are you, Lord?" I asked.

The voice responded, "I am Jesus whom you are persecuting; but rise and enter the city and you will be told what to do."

When I rose, I was blinded. Days later, one of God's servants touched my eyes, spoke to me of Christ, and baptized me.

I spent years pondering these great events, knowing only that peace and joy had come upon me—it came in spite of me, not because of me.

Much later, an old friend, Barnabas, searched and found me in my hometown of Tarsus. He brought me to Antioch to aid in a great work. And oh, the joy and power I felt there! I, who had opposed the Christ, was now able to strengthen the brothers and sisters who loved and followed him.

So you see, last of all as to one untimely born, the risen Christ appeared unto me [1 Corinthians 15:8]. Wherefore I was not disobedient to the heavenly vision [Acts 26:9]. Is not that the birth of Jesus—in me?

PANELIST TWO: That's not what I was driving at. I was wondering—

PAUL: (*again interrupting*) Then let me tell you more birth stories.

(*reliving, reminiscing*) What great days those were in Antioch. People so eagerly received the gospel, then grew strong and firm in the Savior. At Antioch they first used a new term for us—Christ partisans. They later shortened it to Christians, which might be translated "those in whom Christ *has been born*."

Then the Holy Spirit directed that Barnabas and I should do the work for which we were called. We were to go and share

42

the good news of Christ in many places. So set out we did. We traveled the world telling of the coming of the Promised One.

Many were born anew into the everlasting realm. The common folk heard us gladly. By God's grace, we won a demon-possessed slave girl, a jailer, some soldiers, a few prostitutes, many laborers.

Not many of these new believers "were wise according to worldly standards. Not many were powerful, not many were of noble birth; but God chose what is foolish in the world to shame the wise, God chose what is weak in the world to shame the strong. God chose what is low and despised in the world, even things that are not to bring to nothing things that are, so that no human being might boast in the presence of God. . . . Let [anyone] who boasts, boast of God" [1 Corinthians 1:26–31].

(Panelist Two *throws up his or her hands in despair at getting Paul on the subject, but* Panelist One *has become intrigued.*)

PANELIST ONE: You make this sound so exciting. Was there pain, suffering, setbacks?

PAUL: Oh yes. There were dangers aplenty. But the greatest pain came when persons who had chosen Christ, floundered and fell away. Folks in the church in Galatia were among the most troubling to me. I once wrote to those lovable idiots, "My little children, for whom I am again in the pain of childbirth until Christ is formed in you" [Galatians 4:19].

PANELIST TWO: (*guffaws*) *You* are in birth pains over someone until Christ is born again in them? What a mixed-up image!

PAUL: I know. I was beside myself, not thinking very clearly. Thanks be to God, some Galatians responded and allowed Christ to be born, once more, within them.

PANELIST ONE: Let's change the focus of our conversation for a while. Paul, we all love Luke's and Matthew's stories about the birth. Would you tell us what you believe about the birth of Jesus Christ, of his coming into the world?

PAUL: I'd much rather tell you what I believe about the cross of Christ. "[I] preach Christ crucified, a stumbling block to Jews and folly to Gentiles, but to those who are called, both Jews and Greeks, Christ the power of God and the wisdom of God" [1 Corinthians 1:23–24].

PANELIST TWO: (*muttering almost inaudibly*) There he goes again!

PANELIST ONE: (*persisting*) I respect that. But for a moment, won't you tell us what you believe about the *birth* of Christ.

PAUL: (*finally hearing their question, not avoiding it*) I will try. What do I believe about the birth of Christ?

I believe that for centuries, God had been preparing the world for this wonderful birth. "When the fullness of time had come, God sent his Child, born of a woman, born under the law, to redeem [both] those under the law [and those who were not]" [Galatians 4:4]. Because of this birth, we have been adopted in to the family of God. "God has sent the Spirit of God's Child into our hearts, crying, 'Abba! Father!'" [Galatians 4:4–6].

PANELIST ONE: (*recognizes an important spiritual truth*) Abba! Father. Yes. Is there anything else you can tell us?

PAUL: I believe that when Jesus was born, a unique form of the Godhead entered into our lives and world. I greatly love and firmly believe that hymn we used to sing about Christ:

"Let the same mind be in you that was in Christ Jesus, who though he was in the form of God, did not regard equality with God as something to be exploited,

but emptied himself,
    taking the form of a slave,
being born in human likeness.
And being found in human form,
    he humbled himself
and became obedient to the point of death,
even death on a cross.
Therefore God has highly exalted him
    and gave him the name which is above every name,
so that at the name of Jesus
    every knee should bend,
in heaven and on earth and under the earth,
and every tongue confess
    that Jesus Christ is Savior,
to the glory of God." [Philippians 2:5–11]

PANELIST ONE: I like that hymn, too. Thank you, Paul, that was very helpful.

PAUL: Wait, there's more. The birth of Christ!
    I believe that in his coming, living, teaching, dying, rising, he was the very love of God of which he spoke. And he still is.
    "[Jesus] is patient and kind; [Christ] is not arrogant or rude. [Jesus] does not insist on his own way . . . is not irritable or resentful. [Christ] does not rejoice at wrong but rejoices in the right. [Jesus] bears all things, believes all things, hopes all things, endures all things. [The love that came to us in that manger] never ends," and it will not fail [1 Corinthians 13:4–7]. What incredible joy there is when that loving Christ is found among us.

PANELIST ONE: Love. What a fitting conclusion to our conversation. Paul, we thank you for being with us—

PAUL: (again interrupting) Wait, I'm not through. I believe that when Jesus was born he came to a world estranged from God and divided against itself. But he is our peace. He is the one who loves all and whom all can love. He broke down the dividing walls of partition between us. "So then [we] are no longer strangers and sojourners, but [we] are fellow citizens with the saints and members of the household of God" [Ephesians 2:19].

The time we have to live and tell this story is limited. He will come again in power.

As a matter of fact, I've sat around here too long. I must go and tell this story to others, for this is why Christ called me.

(*Ignoring the protest of Panelist One,* Paul *gets up, walks over his marks on the floor, and proceeds out to audience, pantomiming a word of witness here and there as he goes out.*)

PANELIST TWO: (*flustered and almost forgetting she may still be on camera*) Well, I'll be. I've met some strange ones in my day, but he—

PANELIST ONE: (*remembering they are still on camera, touches her colleague's arm in a mildly restraining way, recovers, turns to face "camera" and make a concluding statement*) Today we have had an alternate view of the birth of Christ. Let me attempt to summarize our guest's viewpoint. (*Very quiet music begins in background and slowly builds.*)

He was saying to us the birth of Christ is not merely an ancient occurrence but rather a pivotal point in God's history.

He contended that this event began a worldwide revolution, a new way of relating, loving, and reconciling.

For him, a favorite part of the Christmas story is spiritual rebirth—his and others'.

The viewer may agree or disagree with our guest but will not be able to forget him. Wherever he is, we thank Paul for being with us on *Face the World.* Merry Christmas and good day.

(*The music that has been playing quietly comes up for a conclusion.*)

❋❋❋❋❋❋❋

FOUR

A Bout with the Angels

For Individuals

Imagine. Imagine angels. If angels are God's messengers, stretch your mind to think of all the ways they might be experienced.

Read. Read the various passages in which angels are mentioned in the Christmas narratives. These include Matthew 1:18–25, 2:13–14; Luke 1:8–15, 1:26–38, 2:8–15. Also read Hebrews 13:2.

Pray. Gracious Guide, make your way known among us. We thank you for every expression of your love. We trust your ways to bring fresh revelation, insight, and truth into our lives. Open our hearts. Open our minds. Open our imaginations. In the name of the One announced by angels, Christ our Savior. Amen.

Then *experience the story.*

For Small Groups, Families, and Classes

Plan a Group Reading of the Script. This drama has a three-person cast. Each part is distinct, so you need three readers. There are two aspects of the angels' presence that you will need to decide how to interpret. For one, they have scarves that make them invisible to humans; when these scarves are removed, the angels are visible. Angelo puts his scarf back on at one point to "tell Tom off." You may need to explain that. Also, the angels make a gesture each time they make any reference to God. It can be hands in prayer and an upward look, or any gesture you select.

Twice an "angel choir" sings. You will need to decide whether to have a person sing these lines or to narrate them.

Discuss the Dramatic Story. Here are some possible discussion questions. Question 1 should be discussed before the play has been read; questions 2–4 are to be used after the reading.

1. Break into groups of three or four to talk about the following questions. Recent surveys show that vast numbers of people believe they have seen or sensed the nearness of an angel. Have you ever had such an experience? Have you ever had a person in your life who felt like a gift from God to you? Tell about that person and what she or he meant to you.

2. The angels told some of the Christmas stories from *their* perspective. What did their point of view add to the way you have thought of those stories?

3. If you were an angel, would you be as impatient with human beings as Angelo was? Or do you feel, as Angela did, that humans deserve a little more understanding? Why do you feel the way you do?

4. What hints of deeper meanings of Christmas did you hear in this story? What invitations to a richer observation of Christmas did you receive?

For Those Presenting the Drama in Public

In addition to the guidance already offered, here is information to aid in staging this drama.

Setting. Tom's dining room table. A Saturday night in December.

Cast of Characters

TOM: A bookbound, earthbound Sunday school teacher with heavy spectacles.

ANGELA AND ANGELO: Two playful, rollicking angels who can appear and disappear, be heard or not be heard, and love to play these games. At the same time, they don't ever forget their mission. Angela is upbeat and cheerful, while Angelo can at times be sarcastic.

(*When the play was first performed, the angels were dressed in white tops and black bottoms, with gold-tinsel halos and gold tinsel around black bow ties. They wore large, gauzy scarfs, which they removed to be visible and which Angelo speaks through in one scene. A long, flowing robe, three small sets of wings, and a wand with a star were their only props. Tom had a desk and books.*)

The Drama

The scene opens on an empty room. At one side is a bare table. Shortly, a door opens. Tom *enters, staggering under the load of a huge stack of books.* Angela, *unseen by Tom, follows him a couple steps behind, mimicking his staggering. When a book is about to fall, she straightens it. Still unseen, she helps him set the stack on the table.* Tom *sits.* Angela *stands to one side behind him, quietly amused at his frustration and struggle.*

With a sigh, Tom *opens a book, frantically flips through several pages, and sets it aside. As he reaches for another,* Angela, *still unseen, hands it to him.* Tom *stares at the book, puzzled at how he retrieved it. He turns several pages.*

TOM: That ungrateful class! They said they were bored with the usual Christmas lessons. They had heard it all. I asked them what they wanted to study and they said—

TOM AND ANGELA: (*together*) Angels! Angels!!

ANGELO: (*appears from the other side of the stage*) What have we here?

ANGELA: A teacher. One of those serious types. Studying us.

ANGELO: Tommy, my boy, how many times have you been told not to delay your lesson until Saturday night? (*to Angela*) He looks so desperate. Can we help him?

ANGELA: We're not supposed to do that for frivolous reasons. (Angelo *makes a pleading gesture, adds an "Oh please."*) Oh, all right. (*They remove their "invisible scarves."*)

ANGELO: (*clears his throat loudly but Tom does not notice, then does it again, louder still*) Young man, may we help you?

TOM: (*jumps, shivers*) What? Who are you?

ANGELO: Don't you know, we're— (Angelo *and* Angela *strike "angel poses," one blowing a make-believe herald's trumpet, the other holding and strumming a pretend small harp.*)

TOM: The Salvation Army Band?

ANGELA: You're close.

TOM: Angels?? (Angelo *and* Angela *nod with big smiles.*) I don't believe you!

ANGELA: Why not?

TOM: You don't look like angels.

ANGELA: (*picking up a long beautiful cape and with a flourish putting it on*) Is this better? Angelo doesn't wear one—can't manage stairs with it! (*laughs*)

TOM: That's more like it, but—

ANGELO: You'd prefer us with wings? How many? Two big pretty ones? Or six, as in Isaiah—two to cover our faces, two to cover our feet, and two to fly? (*As he does this, he picks up sets of wings and, with Angela's help, puts one over her feet, one over her face, and one on her back.*)

ANGELA: That passage is more about the glory and majesty of the Almighty (*with any reference to God,* Angelo *and* Angela *make a suitably reverential gesture*) than about how we look.

ANGELO: Many times throughout history, the Eternal (*gesture again*) has sent us as messengers. Most of the time we looked just like you. (*grimaces; he clearly does not think too highly of humans*) People didn't even recognize us.

ANGELA: Here, I will show you. (*Picks up Tom's Bible. With one finger opens it to a place early in Genesis.*) Read this.

TOM: (*reads*) "The angel of God found Hagar by a spring of water in the wilderness" [Gen. 16:7]. (Angela *flips a couple pages;* Tom *reads again.*) "Abraham looked up and saw three men standing near him. . . . he ran to meet them and bowed down and offered hospitality to them" [Gen. 18:2–7].

ANGELO: (*proudly*) We were there! Further, you need to be careful with us, Tommy. Read this. (*flips to New Testament*)

TOM: (*reads*) "Let mutual love continue. Do not neglect to show hospitality to strangers, for by doing that some have entertained angels unawares" [Heb. 13:1–2].

ANGELA: "Angels unawares."

ANGELO: "Angels unawares."

TOM: (*upset, but growing in awareness that maybe he is encountering angels*) Okay, okay, I got it! All right, if you folks *are* angels, there's something I've always wanted to know, but it's kinda personal.

(Angelo *and* Angela *nod and sit near Tom to hear his question. A moment of silence.*)

TOM: Do you exist?

(Angelo *and* Angela *look at each other, puzzled.*)

ANGELO: Do we exist? Do you?

TOM: What I mean is, what are you?

ANGELA: What's the problem, Tom?

TOM: Well, when I read the Bible, it seems to use different terms to talk about the same thing. It speaks about God's loving presence to help us. (Angela *and* Angelo *nod in agreement.*) Then I read about the Holy Spirit to help us. (*Again they affirm.*) And then I read about angels to help us. (*Again nod yes.*) What's the difference among them?

(*There is frustrated silence.* Angelo *and* Angela *look at each other in bewilderment.* Angelo *is rather annoyed.*)

ANGELO: Difference?

ANGELA: (*gently*) Tom, you think like a mortal. We *are* almighty God's (*gesture*) love, praise, and service. Sometimes we are the Eternal's (*gesture*) messengers and agents. Just trust that. You don't need to know that much about us. (Angela *reaches out and puts a reassuring hand on Tom's shoulder. Now Tom is upset. He turns from the reassuring gesture, paces agitatedly.*)

TOM: Oh great! Finally *maybe* I meet angels. And finally *maybe* I can explore the questions I've always wondered about. But these *possible* angels can't even talk to me about important stuff, because we're from such different realms! I'm getting a headache, and I still don't have a lesson for tomorrow. Isn't there any way you can help me understand?

(*They are troubled that he is upset and would genuinely like to help. After a moment's thought, Angelo has an idea.*)

ANGELO: Yes, there might be one. (Tom *looks at him and waits for what he will say.*) Stories. (Angela *brightens and murmurs agreement.*) Stories might bridge the gap. That's what the Almighty (*gesture*) uses to help us understand you.

ANGELA: Would you like stories of what we have been asked to do?

TOM: (*uncertainly*) Well, I guess so.

(Angela *and* Angelo, *relieved that there is some way to communicate, huddle to brainstorm about what stories to tell. One laughs and suggests, "Let's tell him about old Zechariah." The other laughs and agrees.*)

ANGELA: Tom, there was a time when we had several tasks close together because a new day of reconciliation was dawning. The first of those was to an elderly man named Zechariah. He was on his week of service as a priest when I found him. For the first time in his life, the lot had fallen to him to enter the sanctuary and offer incense.

ANGELO: (*now Zechariah*) Wondrous God, what a privilege to enter this holy place, to offer the incense and the prayers. I wish this opportunity would have come when I was young. Then you would have heard our prayers for a child to be a priest after me. But now Elizabeth and I are old and beyond hope.

(Angelo *pantomimes seeing Angela "standing at the honored place beside the altar." He is terrified and drops the incense.*

Throughout the next, he shakes, his voice has tremors, and he becomes more and more awestruck and unable to believe.)

ANGELO: Wh-wh-who are you?

ANGELA: Do not be afraid, Zechariah, your prayer has been heard.

ANGELO: It has not!

ANGELA: Your wife Elizabeth will bear you a son—

ANGELO: She will not!

ANGELA: —and you will call his name John.

ANGELO: We will not!

ANGELA: You will have joy and gladness and many will rejoice at his birth, for he will be great in the sight of God.

ANGELO: He will not!!

ANGELA: (*thoroughly angry*) I thought you were faithful and blameless. I don't know why the Almighty One (*gestures*) wastes effort on such as you. In spite of your faithlessness, what I say *will* happen. (*She grasps his chin.*) And as for you, you will become mute, unable to speak, until the day these things occur. (*She ends strongly, turns with a flourish, and then assumes the role of narrator.*)

ANGELA: (*continuing*) When Zechariah went out and attempted to give the blessing, he *could not speak.*

ANGELO: (*Raises his hands in blessing, and attempts to speak, but no words come. He cannot resist the temptation to break character to give an aside to Tom out of the side of his mouth.*) Angela goofed. We are just supposed to bring the message, not interfere.

ANGELA: (*wilts him with an angry stare, then continues*) After those days his wife Elizabeth conceived. . . . In time the child was born. They named him John, and Zechariah's tongue was loosed. (*sweetly*) Now you may speak.

ANGELO: (*joyously, excitedly, perhaps pantomiming holding the child*)

> Blessed be the Sovereign God of Israel,
> for God has looked favorably on God's people and redeemed
>   them.
> By the tender mercy of our God
> the dawn from on high will break upon us,
> to give light to those who sit in gloom and in the
> shadow of death,
> to guide our feet into the way of peace. (Luke 2:68, 78–79)

ANGELA: The child grew and became strong in spirit.

ANGELO: (*after a pause, to Tom*) That's one story. Would you like to hear another? (Tom *nods, perhaps says "Sure."* Angelo *continues.*) This story is much different. I was sent to a young woman—just a youth, she was. The message was so personal, I sought to find her alone. But she was such a busy person, working hard, talking with her friends, stopping for little chats with Joseph. Finally, one day, I found her at home alone, mixing the bread dough for the next day.

(Angela *anticipates this last line and "becomes" Mary toward the end of Angelo's statement. She is kneeling, holding a bowl in her hand, mixing away. She is humming merrily.*)

ANGELO: (*comes up behind her, speaks a little too loudly*) Hail, O favored one. God is with you.

ANGELA: (*confused, with a bit of sarcasm*) What sort of greeting is that?

ANGELO: Mary, don't be afraid. You *have* found favor with God. And now, you will conceive in your womb and bear a son, and you will name him Jesus. He will be great, the greatest that ever will live. He will found a kingdom of God's rule. Of this kingdom there will be no end.

ANGELA: How can this be? I have no husband.

ANGELO: I know. The Holy Spirit will come upon you, and the power of the Most High will overshadow you; therefore the child to be born will be holy; he will be called Son of God.

(*Throughout this conversation, it becomes ever clearer to Mary what a terrible responsibility she is being asked to accept. Now she speaks of these feelings.*)

ANGELA: A baby without a husband? Will Joseph understand? Will he still respect and love me? Will he still marry me?

ANGELO: (*gently*) Mary, I only bring requests. I don't do forecasts. (Angela *gives him a look that says, "Be good and don't try to be funny."*)

ANGELA: My friends, and the older women, will they still like me and hold me in high regard?

ANGELO: I do not know.

ANGELA: All I've hoped for is a little corner of peace away from all the hatred and war. Will this mean I will be thrust into the midst of all that conflict?

ANGELO: I'm afraid it does.

ANGELA: The child that is to be so wonderful—will the Almighty protect him and keep him from harm?

ANGELO: He will be born fully human into this world with all its risks, hatreds, and jealousies. Your heart and his might break. But through him, God's love will prevail.

ANGELA: (*to herself*) I have been wishing for God's peaceful actions among us—and now I am the one whom God chooses. Cost what it will, I cannot say no. (*to Angelo, with resolve*) Here am I, the servant of God; let it be with me according to your word.

ANGELO: (*walks away, pauses for a moment of silence, then speaks to Tom*) Then the angel departed from her. Heaven stood on tiptoe, cheering Mary on, hoping she would make the right choice. And she did! You might tell your class that story to show how humans should talk to us angels.

(*Sometimes Tom can get into a language of the heart. Other times, his scientific, twentieth-century mind gets in the way. Now it gets in the way.*)

TOM: If that's how humans should talk to angels, how do angels talk to humans? I'm still not sure this conversation is even happening. How do angels communicate with us earthlings?

(Angelo *is disgusted, after all this. He holds up his "invisible scarf" and shouts sarcastically into* Tom's *face. Tom, of course, does not hear this. He "freezes" for this speech, looking right through Angelo.*)

ANGELO: How do angels speak? Usually we talk out loud, direct. But humans are so *dumb*, so *dull*, so *stupid*, that they don't even get it!

ANGELA: Angelo, be nice. (*He grumbles, "Oh, all right," and pulls his "invisible scarf" away.* Angela *snaps her fingers and* Tom *comes out of his "freeze."*) Tom, you wanted to know how angels speak? (*He nods yes.*) We have many ways. We pick the manner that fits the person. Joseph was such a practical man. "What you see is what you get," he used to say. So I spoke to him in his dreams.

By this time Angelo *has sat down and has apparently drifted off to sleep. He snores a bit.* Angela *comes up and speaks quietly in his ear.*) Joseph, son of David, do not be afraid to take Mary as your wife, for the child conceived in her *is* from the Holy Spirit. You will call the child Jesus, for he will save his people from their sins.

ANGELO: (*as Joseph, awakes, stretches, gets up, and speaks excitedly to an imaginary Mary*) Mary, let's not waste any more time. Let's be married at once. And Mary, when the baby is born, let's name him Jesus.

ANGELA: Through dreams, I guided Joseph—through danger, to Egypt, and finally to a quiet home in Nazareth. I spoke to the Magi through a star.

ANGELO: That was a nice touch, Angela.

ANGELA: I needed to find some way to get through to them, with their eyes only on ancient books or in telescopes. They needed to adore the one that binds all peoples, heaven and earth, heart and mind together.

(Angela *holds a star on a wand aloft in one hand, backing, guiding persons along a route with the other hand, while* Angelo *speaks.*)

ANGELO: After they had heard King Herod, "they set out; and there, ahead of them, went the star they had seen at its rising, until it stopped over the place where the child was. When they saw that the star had stopped, they were overwhelmed with joy. On entering the house, they saw the child with Mary his mother; and they knelt down and paid him homage. Then, opening their treasure chests, they offered him gifts of gold, frankincense, and myrrh" (Matt. 2:9b–11).

(*a brief pause*)

ANGELA: I spoke in yet another way to simple shepherds. By now the baby had been born. But Joseph and Mary were alone in Bethlehem. They were so lonely and so frightened that I wanted to give them a party. So I gave the message in a way that could not be missed. I came in a glorious light.

(Angelo *kneels before her, shading his eyes, barely glancing at her.*)

ANGELA: (*continuing*) Do not be afraid, for behold, I bring you good news of great joy for all the people. To you is born this day in the city of David a child who is Christ the Savior. This will be a sign for you: you will find a babe wrapped in swaddling clothes, wrapped in love, and lying in a manger (Luke 2:10–12). (*addressing Tom*) To make sure the truth hit them, I had summoned the angelic choir. And we sang! We sang—
    (*with the help of a chorus*) "Glory to God. Glory to God in the highest."

ANGELO: (*a bit more quietly and reverently than usual, to Tom*) The shepherds did not miss the message. Immediately they came, welcomed the child, provided the welcoming party.

TOM: (*getting caught up in this*) It must be so joyful and peaceful to be an angel, a messenger of God.

(Angelo *and* Angela, *perplexed, look at each other.*)

ANGELO: Joyful? Peaceful? Not often, when you have to deal with hard-of-heart human beings. I remember the worst day of all.

(*In this scene, Angela will portray the "chair-angel" through-out, and Angelo will portray a number of opinions from various angels.*)

ANGELA: Will the heavenly council please come to order. I have assembled you that all may hear of a most disturbing development. Scribe?

ANGELO: (*reading from imaginary scroll*) We just intercepted this order from King Herod's strategy room: "Let a cohort be organized at once to go to Bethlehem and *kill all boy babies* two years old or younger. The new king must be destroyed."

ANGELO: (*In this scene, he portrays a number of angels, working themselves up into a riot. Angela tries to interrupt and get control, until she shouts them down at the climax.*) Chair-angel? I move that we stop this awful plan! . . . Let's give the old geezer some of his own medicine . . . Turn him into a pillar of salt and let the cattle lick him away . . . Let's push his stone palace in on him . . . Put a millstone around his neck and drop him in the deepest part of the *Dead* Sea! . . . Before he hurts that baby or any baby, let's zap him!!!

ANGELA: Angels, angels, *let there be order!* (*to Angelo*) *And you, sit down!!* I feel the same way. (*sighs deeply*) But the Almighty (*gesture*) will not allow it. Our great God (*gesture*) treasures human "freedom" so much that we cannot intervene. They will have to go their wicked stupid ways until they finally receive the Loving One. Even if it takes a thousand years. And it probably will.

ANGELA: (*to Tom*) And so it was. The child did escape and grow to manhood, however.

TOM: Did that finish your part in the coming of Christ?

ANGELA: Oh no. We were at his side all of his days on earth. I ministered to him after he fasted forty days in the wilderness.

ANGELO: I wiped the sweat off his forehead when he prayed in Gethsemane.

ANGELA: I held up his arms as he suffered on a cross.

ANGELO: I stood by his tomb and told the visitors he was not there, but is risen as he said! What a privilege that was!

(*Pause.* Angela *and* Angelo *look at each other and nod. It is time to leave.*)

ANGELA: Tom, it's late and you must rest. We hope your lesson goes well.

TOM: Wait, don't leave me.

ANGELO: (*sarcasm returns*) First he doesn't believe in us, and now he doesn't want us to go.

TOM: I may need more of your help. When will I see you again?

ANGELA: (*warmly*) Tom, we will be with you whenever the Almighty (*gesture*) sends us, whenever you need us. We will be close to you always.

TOM: How will I know you?

ANGELA: You may not. I may be with you in a dream, or a whisper in your ear, or as extra strength when you are at the end of your rope.

ANGELO: I may be sitting in the back row of your class, asking tough questions, or heckling you a bit.

TOM: I believe that!

ANGELA: Remember, Tom—

ANGELA AND ANGELO: (*they say this together while fluidly backing away from him, offstage*) Do not neglect to show hospitality to strangers, for by doing so some have entertained angels unawares.

(Tom *looks at where they have disappeared. The choir again sings, "Glory to God . . . " Slowly his eyes look up. Toward the end of the singing, he picks up his Bible and starts down the middle aisle.*)

FIVE

✲✲✲✲✲✲✲

Privileged Conversation

For Individuals

Imagine. Building on your knowledge of what makes women's friendships special—including women who were pregnant and bore children together, and those who raised children together—imagine the friendship of Mary and Elizabeth from the Gospel stories. After you have visualized it in your own mind, compare your concept with that of the author of this story.

Read. Read Luke 1:39–56. This passage provides all we know about the relationship between Mary and Elizabeth. However, we do also know that Mary outlived her son, and that John and Jesus related to each other and communicated with each other as adults. Therefore, a maturing, long-term friendship is not unreasonable and quite easy to imagine.

Pray. Kind and merciful Parent, you have given so many good and precious gifts. Today we thank you for the gift of friends. Our closest companions help make your love close and real. Such folk add vibrant color and glorious music to our lives. Thank you for friends. In the name of the One who has called us friends, even Jesus the Anointed. Amen.

Then *experience the story.*

For Small Groups, Families, and Classes

Plan a Group Reading of the Script. This is a three-person script. There are two women of different ages and a narrator who can be of either gender. It would be difficult to do justice to the women's parts by sight reading. More so than the others, this play requires some preparation. Keep in mind that this story-drama focuses on the friendship between these two women as they experience and share events that scripture records.

Discuss the Dramatic Story. Here are some possible discussion questions. Question 1 should be discussed before the play is read; questions 2–5 are to be discussed after the reading.

1. In smaller groups of two to four persons, have all of them identify their oldest friend and their best friend (these may or may not be the same person). Ask them to tell about how they became friends, what holds them together, and what in these friendships means the most.

2. What elements were apt to contribute to Mary and Elizabeth's becoming fast friends? What elements would have made it difficult for them to do so?

3. If the conjecture in this story is true—that Jesus' and John's mothers were very good friends—what impact would this have had on their mutual ministry?

4. Someone has said that the deepest friendships are those in which two people "touch souls." In what ways did Mary and Elizabeth touch souls? Have you ever had a friend with whom you touched souls? Would you be willing to tell about it?

5. Do you have enough friendships? Does your church have means to encourage such friendships to mature? If so, what are the ways your church does so? What can you do to find and make such friends and help others to do so?

For Those Presenting the Drama in Public

In addition to the guidance already offered, here is information to aid in staging this drama.

Setting. The home village of Zechariah and Elizabeth in the hill country of Judea, from the months shortly before Jesus' birth to the years of his ministry—a span of some thirty years.

Cast of Characters

NARRATOR

MARY: A wonder-filled, turbulent, pregnant teenager at the beginning who ages to an older midlife woman in the telling of this story. Mary not only ages, but matures and grows in wisdom and faith.

ELIZABETH: A "young old" elderly woman who is also—to her great surprise—pregnant at the beginning of this story. During the story she ages considerably, becomes quite feeble, and dies.

Mary and Elizabeth have a slight relationship at the beginning of the story. This relationship grows and grows into a deeply meaningful and supportive friendship. Persons portraying these two persons should explore ways to express and communicate this deepening relationship, so richly supportive for each. Their friendship grows through telling their stories, expressing feelings—including fear and hope, sharing secrets, and offering support and wisdom.

In the first scene, Mary is a frightened, confused teenager, but she grows in strength through her relationship with Elizabeth, becoming able to face the hardships and take responsibility for her child. Subsequent scenes see this relationship deepening until, in the final scene, it continues even beyond Elizabeth's death.

The Drama

NARRATOR: Today we explore some little-known spaces within well-known stories.

You know the story of Zechariah and Elizabeth, those devout but childless people. You recall that an angel of God appeared to Zechariah and told him that in response to their prayers, they would bear a son who should be called John. Not only would they have a son, but this son would be used mightily of God to turn many to God and make a people fully ready for their God.

65

And, as you recall, Zechariah, who could live with disappointment, could not believe good news. And so he was stricken speechless. However, the promise was kept. In their older years, Elizabeth conceived the promised child. For five months she kept herself secluded, as she said to herself:

ELIZABETH: (*offstage*) How good God is to me now that the shame I have suffered has been taken away by divine will.

NARRATOR: As the child grew within Elizabeth, another quiet but world changing event was taking place. You also know the story of the very young Mary of Nazareth. Probably a teenager, perhaps even an early teenager, Mary was betrothed but not yet married when she too had an angel visitor. The angel told her that she would conceive and bear a son, a most significant son. He would be great, occupy the throne of his forefather David, and have a dominion that would never end.

This was too much for Mary.

MARY: (*offstage*) How can this be? I am not married. I have never been with a man.

NARRATOR: The angel told her that the Holy Spirit would come upon her. The power of the Most High would overshadow her. Lo, her kinswoman Elizabeth, thought barren, was already in her sixth month, for nothing is impossible with God.

Mary must have been excited, filled with wonder and even more filled with fear. Still, she made one of the most brave responses ever known to humankind. She responded:

MARY: (*offstage*) I belong to God, body and soul. Let it happen as you say.

NARRATOR: That's how it began. Two women were called to conceive, carry, deliver, and raise two boys who would be powerfully used of God. That's the well-known part of the story. But for the less familiar part—did you ever wonder where they found the strength and courage to do all that they were called to do? I think I know at least part of the answer. It is this, the lesser-known story, that I will now tell you.

After the angel visited Mary, she was filled with awe and confusion. Whom could she talk to? What should she do about Joseph? Who could be trusted with her secret? Only one person came to mind, her kinswoman Elizabeth, of whom the angel spoke.

And so the teenaged, newly pregnant Mary set out and made the perilous, several-days walk from Nazareth to the Judean hill country where Zechariah and Elizabeth lived.

(*During this speech,* Mary *appears. She is walking a circuitous route, looking very fatigued, stricken with waves of nausea.*)

MARY: I wish I could have let them know I was coming, could have asked if I could stay a while. I hope I don't upset them. (*calls out*) Elizabeth! Zechariah!

(Elizabeth *appears and is overjoyed but not terribly surprised that Mary is here. Elizabeth is six-plus months pregnant. At the beginning she is almost reverential in the way she treats Mary, but she quickly responds to Mary's vulnerability.*)

ELIZABETH: Mary, what a privilege! Blessed are you among women and blessed is the child you will bear!! Yes, (*looking up*) your secret has been revealed to me. (Mary *tries to smile and disguise her faint feeling as* Elizabeth *excitedly goes on.*) I may have felt a little movement before, but when I heard your voice, the child within me jumped for joy!

MARY: Please, may I have some water? And a little bread, perhaps?

ELIZABETH: You poor child, sit down. I will bring you much more than that. You are eating for two now! (*brings baskets of food*) Have some fresh fruit and some of these salt fish.

MARY: (*catches the smell of the fish, winces and turns away*) A little fruit maybe.

ELIZABETH: (*smiling, compassionate*) I'd almost forgotten about the morning sickness and the nausea. I keep a pot of bitter herb tea that's just the thing. (*Brings her a cup.* Mary *sips and grimaces.*) I know it tastes awful, but it will settle you, just like that. (Mary *sips more and does begin to feel better.*)

MARY: How long will the nausea last?

ELIZABETH: A few months—it will be better soon. I will keep the tea ready for any time you need it.

MARY: And the awful tiredness?

ELIZABETH: That will be better soon as well. Rest as much as you want to.

MARY: I am feeling better already. I needed you so, Elizabeth. I haven't dared talk to anyone about pregnancy. And of course, I could say nothing about the *angel*!

ELIZABETH: Mary, tell me all that is on your heart. I want to hear every word.

MARY: I have questions aplenty. I have been so lonely with them. Even worse, I could tell no one of my joy.

ELIZABETH: You can tell me—I share your joy.

MARY: (*this speech is poetic, like a hymn*) Oh Elizabeth,

my heart is overflowing with praise of my God;
my soul is full of joy in my Savior.
For God has remembered me, lowly servant that I am—and
    remembered you, too.
Generations beyond us will call us blessed.

(*Returns to prose*) Oh, Elizabeth, I can barely imagine all that
God is going to do through our sons!

ELIZABETH: I'm old enough to be your mother. But I feel so
close to you because God is using both of us. And we have this
women's work (*touches both their stomachs*) to do!

MARY: Elizabeth, may I stay with you for a while?

ELIZABETH: I'll need to check with Zechariah, but I am sure you
can. It will be nice to have someone to talk to. Zechariah doesn't
say anything.

MARY: Men! Joseph doesn't say much either. Are all men like that?

ELIZABETH: I guess you did not know. The angel struck
Zechariah speechless when announcing our child's birth. He
has only written or signed messages ever since. (Mary *gestures
apology.*) Oh, it's all right. We'll take our chances with this
wonder. I'm sure he'll be glad to have you stay with us.

NARRATOR: Mary indeed stayed with them for about three
months. What excitement and happiness they felt together!
They prepared for the children, weaving coverings, sewing
swaddling cloths and clothing. (*As the Narrator says this,*
Elizabeth *and* Mary *pantomime these actions.*)

ELIZABETH: (*holds up imaginary baby outfit*) Mary, I've almost
finished the robe he will wear on his presentation day. What do
you think?

MARY: (*laughs aloud*) So big! You must think he will be born full-grown, ready to preach the moment he is born!

ELIZABETH: (*smiles*) Maybe I did overdo it a little. At least it will be big enough. How's yours coming? (Mary *holds up hers.*) Oh Mary, it's beautiful. He will feel your love from the very first moment. (*They reach out and hold each other's hands.*)

NARRATOR: Their favorite time was the end of the day. When all the work was done, they would put up their aching feet, relax, talk, and dream. (*They get into such a relaxed position.*)

MARY: Do you know what I hope, Elizabeth?

ELIZABETH: What?

MARY: I hope that when our sons have done all the wonderful things God plans for them, that they will still have time to sit and relax and be friends, just like you and I are now.

ELIZABETH: I hope so too, Mary. At times I fear for them. These are cruel and dangerous times. I hope they will be safe.

MARY: We know they will overcome. God is with them—and us. I need to remember that. Sometimes I am afraid of having this baby.

ELIZABETH: God is with us as well, Mary. Our Lord will see us through.

NARRATOR: Their days together passed quickly.

ELIZABETH: (*calling Mary from a short distance;* Mary *comes at once*) Mary. I'll make a deal with you. If you will rub my swollen ankles and legs, I will brush your hair!

MARY: Why don't we each rub the other's ankles *and* brush each other's hair! (*They start to do this, talking as they do.*)

ELIZABETH: Mary, my time is close. You need to be back with your people. I'll miss you so, but it *is* time for you to go to them.

MARY: I know. After three months, you'd think we'd be talked out! But you're right. It *is* time.

ELIZABETH: There's a caravan going your way on the morrow. Zechariah and I will pay so that you may travel more safely and ride the wagon when you need to on your return.

MARY: You are so kind. (*Pauses. There is something troubling her. She blurts it out.*) Elizabeth, what do I tell Joseph?

ELIZABETH: That's why you dread returning isn't it? (Mary *nods and looks down.*) Mary, you tell him the truth. You have nothing to be ashamed of. Tell him what actually happened. It may be that God will give Joseph the way to believe you.

MARY: (*bursts into tears and throws herself into Elizabeth's arms*) What if he doesn't believe me? What if we are through?

ELIZABETH: (*holds her*) God will provide, dear one. I wish I had more I could tell you, but I only know that God will provide. (*They hold this position for a moment and then stand and turn their backs to the audience while the* Narrator *speaks.*)

NARRATOR: And so the next day, they said their loving goodbyes, shed a few tears of farewell, and returned to their separate worlds. They hoped to see each other again, quite soon. After all, Judea was only a four- or five-day walk from Galilee. Certainly there would be visits to Jerusalem, or other reasons to be together. Such friendship should not be wasted!

However, life rarely happens the way one expects. It was more than four years before they saw each other again. When that day finally came, they had so much to tell.

(Mary *and* Elizabeth *stand arm in arm looking at their children—a short distance away. They turn to each other from time to time, but their attention is focused on the children.*)

MARY: Oh Elizabeth, John is so big and strong already. And so healthy!

ELIZABETH: I think he was born loving the outdoors! I can hardly get him inside even to eat. He is so strong-willed, so independent. Jesus is a friendly, open child.

MARY: He is so much fun. And question upon question—he never runs out of them. My head spins at the end of the day sometimes. But I wouldn't miss a minute of it.

ELIZABETH: I like the way Jesus met me and greeted me. John isn't that way. He avoids people. He likes to be alone. I worry about that sometimes. I'm surprised at how quickly he took to Jesus.

MARY: Well, we did decide they'd be friends before they were born, remember? (*They both laugh quietly with deep delight.*)

ELIZABETH: John wants to take Jesus to his favorite places in the hills. Is that all right?

MARY: Yes, Jesus, you may go. Joseph, will you go with them and keep an eye on them?

(*Now* Mary *and* Elizabeth *face each other.*)

ELIZABETH: Joseph's being here answers one big question I have. He must have believed you, Mary.

MARY: Not at first. I did what you said: I went back and told him the truth. It was so hard to do. He just couldn't believe such a story. He was so hurt and upset. I hardly blamed him. Even then, he was kind to me. He wasn't going to make a public fuss, but divorce me quietly. Oh, Elizabeth, I loved him so as he struggled in those painful days, but there was nothing I could do.

ELIZABETH: What convinced him?

MARY: God's messenger, in a dream. The moment he awoke from that dream, the tension between us disappeared. It's been strange—not your usual marriage. We've been guided step by step ever since. But tell me about you. How was it when John was born?

ELIZABETH: They call it *labor* with good reason! I had a long, difficult delivery, Mary. The midwife said I could expect that, at my age. While I was in labor, I could hear all my friends and neighbors waiting outside. Their presence was a great comfort to me.

MARY: Did you hurt? Were you afraid?

ELIZABETH: Not more than I could bear. At the most difficult moments, I did remember that this was God's promise.

MARY: How did you feel when he was born and you saw him?

ELIZABETH: Relieved, and then exhausted! I leaned back and slept. Once in a while I woke just enough to hear the music and the dancing at the celebration outside. I was at peace. But what about you? I only heard that you and Joseph left Nazareth and never came back.

MARY: We're on our way back to Nazareth now. It's been quite a journey.

ELIZABETH: I want to hear every bit of it. How was your delivery?

MARY: Unusual—like everything else in my life since that angel appeared. I was almost at full term, when the decree went out for everyone to go to their own town to be registered and taxed. For Joseph that was Bethlehem. There was nothing to do but pack up and go.

ELIZABETH: Poor child. How did you ever stand it?

MARY: Joseph did his best. He bought a donkey for me to ride—a donkey with the sharpest backbone and the roughest walk you could imagine. I was so uncomfortable riding that I'd walk for a while. And then I'd get so weary walking that I'd ride. But it was slow! I'd hoped we could stop overnight here with you, but we had to press on. We didn't want to be fined for being late.

ELIZABETH: Did you make it?

MARY: To Bethlehem, yes. To decent lodging, no. Everything was crowded full when we got there. Finally a kind innkeeper's wife saw that I was pregnant and let us stay in their stable.

ELIZABETH: (*caringly indignant*) A stable! In your condition?

MARY: We were grateful for any place. I was so sore and full of aches the last few miles, I didn't even realize I was already in labor. As soon as we settled in, the pains came on in earnest.

ELIZABETH: All alone?

MARY: It started that way. Joseph tried to help, but he was worse than nothing. So clumsy, so fearful. He isn't even a shepherd that might know something about birth—he's a carpenter.

ELIZABETH: How did you ever manage?

MARY: Joseph was so desperate he ran shouting for help. The innkeeper's wife was so kind. She called for the midwife. Several women gathered close. Their strength fed my soul and I gave birth to my child.

ELIZABETH: Was the labor long and hard?

MARY: (*smiling*) No. (*smiling in recollection*) The midwife said the donkey ride must have jogged him loose! It was soon over. I hardly remember the pain—but oh, the joy when they wrapped him and put him in my arms. I wanted to keep him there forever! Then I wasn't tired at all—I was thrilled and didn't want to miss a thing.

ELIZABETH: It must have been lonely to give birth away from your home. You missed out on having a party and friends to celebrate with you.

MARY: Oh Elizabeth, God provided the party for us! As I lay there, I thought I heard the most beautiful music in the distance. Then I guessed maybe it was just a breeze, or my imagination. But very shortly a band of shepherds came. They were so excited, saying that angels had spoken to them of the birth. The angels had even sung God's praises in my son's honor! That was our band!!

ELIZABETH: (*with quiet delight*) A party of shepherds and angels!

MARY: Those shepherds were so enthusiastic they told everyone, and soon many in the village gathered round. It was a party to remember. I hold it all in my heart.

ELIZABETH: That was nice, but if you only could have been home, people would have given you a party and would have brought gifts for the baby.

MARY: (*laughing out loud*) God provided a celebration as well. A few days later, distinguished rulers from the East came looking for Jesus. They fell on their faces and worshiped him! Then they gave him mysterious and beautiful gifts. Oh Elizabeth, Joseph had borrowed some tools and was doing odd jobs just to buy some food and a place to stay till we could travel back. And they brought us—gold! and frankincense! and myrrh!! Gifts for a king! Of course, that's what he is, my little king.

ELIZABETH: What an adventure! I suppose you're going to tell me that God provided family at his presentation in the Temple.

MARY: (*almost shouts*) Yes! Two wonderful old people had been praying and waiting for the Promised One. God revealed to their hearts who Jesus was. They held him and kissed him, and praised God that they lived to see him. No grandparents could have loved him more. (*frowns*) The old man also told me that because of him, a sword would pierce my heart. Even with that, it was a wonderful day! Oh Elizabeth, God provided everything we needed, including the joy!

ELIZABETH: (*absorbs this, then changes subject*) Mary, where have you folks been? I inquired of you with friends from Nazareth, but no one had heard a thing. You left for Bethlehem, and then it was as if you had disappeared from the face of the earth!

MARY: We've been in Egypt. An angel warned Joseph in a dream that we were in danger. So we fled during the night. The treasured gifts and Joseph's hard work kept us fed in Egypt. Finally the dream angel told Joseph it was safe to come back, and so here we are. We're on our way back to Nazareth.

ELIZABETH: I'm glad you're back, and that you're safe. I've missed you so. Zechariah speaks now—some—but it's not like talking with you. I've always thought of you as a daughter, but we've become like—like sisters, like "young" (*making fun of herself, smoothing her hair*) mothers together! Keeping up with John has given me a new lease on life!

MARY: Oh Elizabeth, isn't it so exciting to have these two little boys to hug and hold?

ELIZABETH: —and let go. Don't forget, Mary, God lent them to us for a few years. They were born to be set free to serve.

MARY: You're right, but I don't want to think of that yet. Look, here they come. Let's see what treasures they found in the hills.

(*They pantomime looking at their children's "treasures"— rocks, flowers, bugs—for a moment as the* Narrator *speaks and then stand with backs to audience awaiting the next scene.*)

NARRATOR: The treasures were not only in the children's hands. There were even greater gifts in the mothers' friendship.

How they loved those all-too-infrequent times together. They would tell their stories, listen to each other's fears and hopes, offer advice and support. Theirs was a link of mother to mother, and it was even more. It was a bond of those who heard God's call and risked themselves in responding.

The years went by.

From time to time, when Joseph and Mary went to celebrate Passover in Jerusalem, they would stop and visit with Zechariah and Elizabeth. One such visit took place eight years later.

MARY: (*hurried and impatient, but excited*) Elizabeth! Elizabeth!! (Elizabeth *appears. She has aged a good bit and walks with a cane. For now, Mary does not notice.* Elizabeth *gestures for her to be seated and offers food.* Mary *continues.*) We can only stay an hour or so. We are *so far* behind the others, and Joseph must be back to work soon, but I *just had* to tell you about what happened.

ELIZABETH: Surely you can sit for a while and tell me all about it. My, you are excited. What did happen?

MARY: As you know, Joseph and I often go to Jerusalem for Passover. Up to now, we have left the children behind with friends. This year it was different. Jesus is twelve, so we brought him for his bar mitzvah. He read Torah for the priests and became a son of the law.

ELIZABETH: (*thinks this is what Mary came to tell*) Our little boys have become men! What an important time in a mother's life!

MARY: (*wrapped up in her own story*) It was such a special occasion. And then the fright of our lives!!

ELIZABETH: What fright? What are you telling me?

MARY: When it was time to return, I left in the early group with the women, and Joseph left in the later group with the men. We all met at sundown to camp for the night. Only then did we realize that Jesus was with neither of us! We were terrified. Had he been kidnaped? Was he lost or hurt?

ELIZABETH: What did you do?

MARY: We went back and looked everywhere for him—for days. The marketplace, the streets; we asked vendors, street entertainers, anyone we could find. We asked and asked. No one had seen him.

ELIZABETH: But you found him?

MARY: Yes, finally. In the last place we looked—it should have been the first—the *Temple*. There he was, listening and asking question after question. I could tell that folks were amazed at his understanding and his answers.

But I was in no mood to listen. I was both so relieved he was alive and *so angry* that he did this to us. He may be a man by law, but he's still my little boy. For once in my life I could have taken a switch to him.

ELIZABETH: What did you do?

MARY: I went right up to him. I tried to keep my voice calm, but he knew what I was feeling. I said, "Son, why have you done this to us? Your father and I have been terribly worried trying to find you." He had a strange, faraway look in his eyes and he answered, "Why did you have to look for me? Didn't you know that I had to be in my Father's house?" Elizabeth, he said "my Father's house"! More and more, he understands who he is and why he is here.

ELIZABETH: I'm not surprised. What happened then? Did he come back with you?

MARY: Oh yes. After that one moment, he was our little boy again, happy to be with us, glad to be found. He's with Joseph now. (Elizabeth *looks faint and wipes her forehead.*) Elizabeth, are you all right?

ELIZABETH: Some days are not as good as others, but I'm okay. Mary, this was not only a time of awakening for Jesus. It was also an important discovery for you. You know that, don't you?

MARY: A discovery for me?

ELIZABETH: Yes. For you. It is a reminder that our children are not our children. They are a loan from God—especially *our* children. We must be willing to let them go.

MARY: Oh Elizabeth, I'm still not ready for that.

ELIZABETH: (*gently but firmly*) Then get ready. As for us, John is more and more on his own, wandering, brooding, praying out in the wilderness. I don't know if he will leave me first, or if I will leave him. I think my time is near.

MARY: (*The full meaning of what Elizabeth is saying comes to Mary and she does not want to hear it!*) Elizabeth, don't say that. You're the best friend I've ever had. I don't know if I could go on without you.

ELIZABETH: Mary, Mary, all we've shared will give you strength. Think of how blessed I am. These last years of my life have been the richest of all. We have been so privileged. When my time comes, I will depart in peace, for my eyes have seen God acting to bring salvation to the world.

(*Lightens up*) And now I must let you go. After losing Jesus, they don't want to lose you! Mary, whether in this world, or in that eternal realm of love, we will meet again!

(*They embrace for a long moment. Then* Elizabeth *gestures that Mary should go.* Mary *starts out, turning to wave every few steps. When Mary is gone,* Elizabeth *turns and walks offstage.*)

NARRATOR: Years passed. Lives changed. Zechariah died, and then Elizabeth, as she had predicted, and then Joseph too, quite unexpectedly. John meditated in the wilderness and Jesus cared for the family carpentry business.

Then the time was at hand. John preached a baptism of repentance in the wilderness. Jesus went to hear and was among the first to be baptized. Through fasting, temptation, and prayer, God's purpose for him came ever more clear.

After John was arrested, Jesus appeared, telling people to repent, calling disciples, and inviting people into the realm of God, which he said was at hand.

For Mary, at times Jesus' ministry was a delight, and other times it was a vexation. The Bible describes at least a few weeks when it held no joy for her. Jesus' family, including

Mary, heard rumors about Jesus. They said he was not eating or drinking. Indeed people were saying he was beside himself, out of his mind, gone mad. Mary tried to take him home for a rest, but he would not go.

A short time later they came to see him again. This time he was busy with a crowd. A message was sent to him, "Your mother, brothers, and sisters are outside asking for you." He responded, "Who are my mother and brothers and sisters? You are! Whoever does what God wants is my brother, my sister, my mother" [Mark 3:20–21, 31–35].

The family was angry. Mary's life was in an uproar. She desperately needed a talk with her wise friend Elizabeth. In desperation, she did the only thing that occurred to her. She traveled to Elizabeth's tomb. In this place, she hoped to remember, to feel her friend's presence and strength, to receive wisdom, and find her way.

MARY: (*kneeling by Elizabeth's tomb*) Almighty One, bless thy servant Elizabeth and give her a special place in your realm— and, O God, preserve her memory as I do gratefully. Amen.

(*She rises, sits by the tomb, and starts talking to Elizabeth—to the tomb, to her memory of Elizabeth.*)

Oh Elizabeth, how I long for one of our good talks. I need you so! When Jesus began his work, I did not hold back. I set him free. It was hard, but I remembered. I did just what you said. After all, some women give up their children to marriage; I gave mine to the reign of God.

I *did* think we'd still be family—that he'd come home for holidays, that we could go see him once in a while. But it's not that way at all. He's disowned us.

The other day we went and asked for him, and he said we *weren't his family*—but just about *everyone else was*! His brothers and sisters said he disgraced us and want nothing more to do with him.

But Elizabeth, I can't let go that easily. Ever since that angel's visit, I've risked too much to let it all end this way—in bitterness.

What should I do? (*Though there is silence it is as though she is hearing a suggestion.*) Do you think that is it? That just as the angel gave me my first call, Jesus' words were my *second call.* Let's see—what were his exact words?—"Whoever does the will of God is my brother and sister and mother."

(*With dawning insight*) You may be right. My calling is to go back as a disciple—a disciple who is also his mother. I'll do that. (*With resolve*) I shall ask no particular favors or recognition. And yet no one loves him more than I do.

(*With even more resolve*) I will be there for him, be with him to face anything he has to face. He will know he has *one person* who won't let him down. It won't be easy. But at least in this way I can finish what I was called to do.

Elizabeth, you always were such a good listener. I hope you think I am doing all right. I miss you so much! God bless and keep you until God grants that we meet again. (*She rises and leaves.*)

NARRATOR: Scripture records that Mary did just that. She affirmed and supported his ministry . . . was at his side when he died . . . was part of the Jerusalem church. Then she vanishes from the pages of history.

You see, Christmas is more than a baby in a manger in dim blue light. It is everyday people risking all in dangerous times to respond to the call of God, lending love and support to each other as they do so. God used these everyday people, guiding their paths, empowering their deeds and their friendships. Through the means of such folks as we have met this morning, a savior was born, grew to manhood, and redeemed the world. Because of such as these, we are able to sing, "Joy to the world, the Savior's come!"

SIX

✦✦✦✦✦✦✦

The Hopeful Waiters— The Waiting Hopers

For Individuals

Imagine. Imagine yourself in your older years, with wonderful secrets in your heart. Imagine what it is like to wait year after year for the secret promises to be fulfilled. Imagine what it is like on the wonderful day that secret promise is kept—and what it is like the day after.

Read. Read Luke 2:22–39.

Pray. God of the morning of life, the noontime of life, the twilight of life, be with us. Give us the gift of memory to recall Your promises to us. We ask also for the gift of faith to claim Your secrets and promises in our later years. We thank You that whatever joys we have known, there is an even greater glory to be revealed. In the name of the Promised One. Amen.

Then *experience the story.*

For Small Groups, Families, and Classes

Plan a Group Reading of the Script. This is a three-person cast—a narrator, an elderly man, and an elderly woman. There are two challenges in doing a play reading of this script. For one, the

Narrator is envisioned as someone who sings some verses of carols at one point and provides background music at another point. Also, the script calls for a choir to sing "For Unto Us a Child Is Born" at the end. You can have someone sing (and hum) these parts, or simply speak them.

The other challenge to reading this play is that there is an elaborate pantomime with few or no words when Simeon and Anna first see the Christ child. You will need to decide whether to pantomime this scene or to do a narration.

Discuss the Dramatic Story. Here are some possible discussion questions. Question 1 should be discussed before the play is read; questions 2–5 are for discussion after the reading.

1. Invite each person to respond—what was the hardest waiting you ever did? For what were you waiting? How long did you have to wait?
2. In what ways were Simeon and Anna like older people that you know and love? In what ways were they different?
3. Every person has a past and a story to tell about that past. What was Anna's story? What was Simeon's?
4. What did seeing the Promised One mean to each of them?
5. How will their experience enrich your Christmas?

For Those Presenting the Drama in Public

In addition to the guidance given earlier, here is some information to help in staging the drama.

Cast of Characters

NARRATOR: As the play is envisioned, the Narrator is one who can sing while playing the piano. This person can then tell part of the story from the piano bench. However, the part could be divided into three— Singer, Pianist, and Speaking Narrator.

SIMEON: An old man, retired. Basically he is a good-natured, devout spirit. At times, however, he can be a bit edgy and sarcastic. He is rather rigid in his habits. At his best, he is a person of deep faith.

ANNA: An old woman, called a prophetess by Luke. She is a cheerful, generous spirit, outgoing and extro-verted, very kind. She loves to talk and sometimes talks when she should be listening.

Put on these characters and enjoy them. Ad-lib lines if it helps you "feel into" the character. Let these be vibrant older people, folks to admire. They should not be stereotyped or trivialized as old peo-ple. Since this is largely a "sit and talk" drama, movement needs to be developed. Find times for Simeon or Anna to rise, move, pace a bit.

Setting. The outer courts of the Temple in Jerusalem. In visualiz-ing where the story takes place, it will help you to know that this part of the Temple (almost certainly the "Court of the Women") is basically a gathering place. Those who are there can see when a couple comes to make the offering for their firstborn son. However, this is a place of activity. There is no need for quiet whispers. Normal conversation, with actors aware of other things going on around them is what is envisioned.

The Drama

NARRATOR: (*plays a bit of "Spirit of God, Descend Upon My Heart" then sings the following verse*) "I ask no dream, no prophet ecstasy, no sudden rending of the veil of clay, no angel visitant, no opening skies, but take the dimness of my soul away."

(*Speaks*) Today I will tell you a quiet, gentle Christmas story. This story has no magnificent star, no bright angel, no mighty chorus. It simply has two older people whose waiting souls were windows into their hearts. Every time I think of them, it takes the dimness of my own soul away.

"Now there was a man in Jerusalem whose name was Simeon, and this man was righteous and devout, looking for the consolation of Israel" [Luke 2:25].

SIMEON: What a wonderful day to be alive! My hip doesn't even hurt too bad. (*prays spontaneously with a gesture of prayer: arms upstretched, eyes heavenward, hands in an open, receiving position*) God, I praise you that I may spend this day in your temple. (*freezes in this position as the narrator speaks*)

NARRATOR: "And it had been revealed to him by the Holy Spirit that he should not see death before he had seen the Messiah" [Luke 2:26].

SIMEON: (*continuing his prayer*) Almighty One, I don't mean to rush you, but wouldn't it be wonderful if today were the day? Nevertheless, I will wait as long as you give me breath. Your mercy is everlasting. Amen.

NARRATOR: "And there was a prophetess, Anna, the daughter of Phanuel, of the tribe of Asher; she was of great age. She had been married for only seven years and was now eighty-four years old" [Luke 2:36, mixed versions].

(Anna *appears down below. She will need to complete "climbing the holy hill" to the temple and coming up the temple steps while* Simeon *speaks.*)

SIMEON: (*waving broadly and calling to her at a distance*) Anna! Up here! I have saved our places. (*confiding to the audience*) That's my friend Anna. I admire her. She's had so much sorrow, and she's all alone in this world. Yet you'd never know it. She's such a sunny, cheerful person. She keeps me going.

ANNA: (*similarly confiding to the audience*) There's my friend Simeon. I like him! A few years ago he hurt his hip and had to leave his beloved hills and flocks. Now he lives with his daughter, her husband, and their four children. Some days he's crabby and hurts my feelings. I try to remember that those are the days the pain is bad, and I try to make allowances. Usually, though, he's a kind, gentle person.

SIMEON: (*as Anna struggles up the steps*) Come on, Anna, you can do it. (*reaches down and gives her a hand with the last few steps*)

ANNA: (*Puffs to get her breath and then delivers these lines, a favorite speech she repeats often. She likes it and smiles broadly as she says it, but it annoys Simeon.*) I do not praise God for the long, steep climb up the holy hill. But I do praise God for the wonderful view when I arrive. I do not praise God for the many steps, but I do praise God that I can still climb them!

SIMEON: (*trying to change the subject*) You're here early today.

ANNA: When I awoke I felt so alone. I wanted to be where the people are and the prayers can be said. It is better when I am here. I can take my turn with the Sisters of Mercy. I can pray for the consolation of our people. You are here *very* early today.

SIMEON: My daughter's small lodging felt so crowded, what with the seven of us. I left as soon as I could, to get out of their way. (*breathing deeply*) I like it here early in the morning, when everything has been scrubbed, before they bring in the animals for the day.

ANNA: Yes, it does smell much better now, doesn't it? Did you bring your lunch? (Simeon *nods*) What did you bring today?

SIMEON: What I always bring—a slab of goat's cheese and a small loaf. And you?

ANNA: I finished my fast at sundown last evening. I found the most delicious dates and figs in the market.

SIMEON: I suppose you will be nibbling on them all day.

ANNA: What does it matter? I always offer some to you. And, I must say, I am rather hungry after my fast. Shall we have a little snack right now, a few bites of our lunches?

SIMEON: I never eat until the sun is high in the sky. High in the sky!

ANNA: Oh Simeon, you're so . . . so regular— (*She smiles and chuckles a bit. There is a comfortable silence for a moment.*)

SIMEON: Anna, did I ever tell you about the time I saved my flock from the sudden storm?

ANNA: You mean that time you were out in the open by yourself, and the unexpected storm with thunder, lightning, rain, and hail came up all at once? (Simeon *grimaces*) Yes, but I'd love to hear it again. (Simeon *makes a hand gesture that he won't repeat it.*) Simeon, did I ever tell you how I met my husband? (*To each of these questions,* Simeon *answers, "Many times," or "Yes," or simply nods vigorously.*) Did I tell you how happy we were? Did you know he was a mason? Do you know about the beautiful little house he built for us? Did I tell you about the accident when he died? Did I tell you that I thought my heart would break? . . . Simeon, after all the years that we have sat and talked, do you suppose there is anything we haven't told each other?

SIMEON: (*uneasily*) Is there anything I haven't told you? Yes, there is one thing I haven't told anyone. I've thought of telling you, but I was afraid you'd think I was a foolish old man. (*quietly*) If I tell you, do you promise not to laugh at me?

ANNA: (*gently and sincerely*) I promise. I'd love to hear your secret, Simeon.

SIMEON: (*remembering, reliving*) When I was out with my flocks I just knew God was all about. Had to be! Things were so beautiful, and at times so powerful!

ANNA: Like the storm you told me about.

SIMEON: Yes. When I was hurt and had to leave my beautiful hills and valleys I was discouraged. To depend on others! To have to live in the city!! I almost despaired of life itself.

ANNA: I remember. That was when I met you.

SIMEON: That was when I started coming to the Temple—one place I didn't crowd others, one place where no one asked me to leave. . . . I'm afraid I wasn't very good company when first you spoke to me.

ANNA: I understood, for I too have known pain and loneliness.

SIMEON: Gradually I decided to seek the God of the hills here in the city—maybe I could find God right here at the Temple?

ANNA: I think your search was successful. I could see the change taking place.

SIMEON: Anna, there is more. (*He gives a silent signal, and their heads come close together for his secret.*) One day, right at this very spot during my morning prayers, the Holy Spirit spoke within me! I didn't hear a thing with my ears, and yet I know the Spirit spoke. (*getting even more quiet and confidential, Anna leaning even nearer*) The Spirit told me that I should not see death before I see the Messiah!! (*At this,* Anna *puts her head back and laughs uproariously. She utters a little "Praise*

God" in her laughter. Simeon *is hurt and offended.*) You promised not to laugh at me.

ANNA: (*reaches out and takes Simeon's hands*) Simeon, dear friend, I'm laughing *with* you. Laughing for joy. You see, God's spirit spoke within me and told me the day of redemption is near. I too have been watching and hoping with great eagerness. Simeon, we share the same hope.

(*As the* Narrator *begins singing, for the first part of the song, they remain in a close secret sharing posture, with the joy of expectation on their faces.*)

NARRATOR: (*singing*)

"Come, thou long expected Jesus,
Born to set thy people free;
From our fears and sins release us;
Let us find our rest in thee."

(*Speaking*) And so they waited for the consolation of Israel.

(*As the* Narrator *begins to sing,* Simeon *and* Anna *move to standing positions, facing the audience. The joy leaves their faces. The strain of waiting comes gradually as the song goes on.*)

NARRATOR: (*continuing to sing*)

"Israel's strength and consolation,
Hope of all the earth thou art;
Dear Desire of ev'ry nation,
Joy of every longing heart."

(*Speaking*) And their waiting went on and on.

(*As the Narrator continues, the strain of waiting shows even more.* Simeon *and* Anna *go to the spots where they began the* first scene—Simeon about to offer his morning prayer, Anna coming from below.)

NARRATOR: (*continuing to sing*)

"As the years fade into darkness
How we long to see thy light.
Though we nearly faint with waiting,
Come, O God, reveal thy might." [new words]

(*Speaking*) And still they waited.

SIMEON: (*in Temple, attempting his daily prayers, though obviously in a much more sour and somber mood*) God, it's a pretty good day. I guess I don't need to tell you, who knows all, that my hip is hurting really bad today. Not only that, the shadows of my life grow longer. I don't have much time left. And still the promise waits. Did I deceive myself? Or did you really speak within me? God, I'm tired of waiting!! But I will continue to wait and pray—not much choice. Amen. (*sees Anna, waves and calls to her, with much less enthusiasm*) Anna, up here.

ANNA: (*She puffs up the steps, but Simeon does not give a hand. She tries to be her bubbly self, but there is a strain of waiting in her as well.*) I do not praise God for the long steep climb up the holy hill. But I do praise God for the wonderful view when I arrive. I do not praise God for the many steps, but I do praise God that I can still climb them.

(Simeon *scowls and mimics her, mouthing the words as she says them. Fortunately, she is looking away and does not see. Anna starts to sit in a different place.*)

SIMEON: (*rather gruffly*) Anna, sit where you always do.

ANNA: Oh, Simeon. (*Modest teasing, but she does what he asks.*

She catches her breath for a few moments, then continues) Any sign? Anything new?

SIMEON: (*This question annoys him, too. On this morning, practically everything does.*) No. No sign. No clue. No developments. Still we wait and wait.

ANNA: Simeon, how do you think we will know the Promised One?

SIMEON: (*even more annoyed*) Anna, we have spoken of this a thousand times. I don't know! Perhaps we will see a man and know, or a youth, or a child. Maybe God will send a woman to deliver us. I doubt that God will send one from the rich, or the mighty, or the powerful, or the priests, but *I just don't know how we will know!*

ANNA: If I upset you so much, maybe I should leave you alone. I'll go see if the Sisters of Mercy need any help. (*rises to leave*)

SIMEON: (*a little softer*) Anna, don't go. I'm sorry. It really is better to share the secret, to wait together. But some days it is so hard.

ANNA: (*reaches out and pats Simeon's hands*) I know. I feel the same way. (*pauses a moment then has a happy thought*) Maybe you'd feel better if you told me about the time you rescued your flock from the flood.

SIMEON: (*cross and sputtering again*) Flood!! It was no flood! I rescued them from a storm, a *storm!!*

ANNA: Of course, a storm. Tell me about it.

SIMEON: (*reluctantly, thinking it won't help, but doesn't have a better plan, so starts without enthusiasm*) I don't think it will help, but I don't have anything else to do, but *wait!* I guess I may as well tell it again. It was a meadow with deep, good grass, and the day was absolutely clear, when all of a sudden storm clouds blew up, in a very brief time . . . (*drifts off, stops, staring at something offstage*)

ANNA: Simeon, what is it?

SIMEON: (*in awe, almost a whisper, still looking*) Over there. (*pointing*) The promise is fulfilled.

ANNA: Who? The father? The mother?

SIMEON: No. The baby.

ANNA: The baby! Of course—our God brings us consolation in a lovely baby. Oh Simeon, let's go to them and tell them we know!

SIMEON: Wait! Let them perform their rites according to the law. (Simeon *and* Anna *watch in wonder as the* Narrator *speaks.*)

NARRATOR: "And when the time came for their purification according to the law of Moses, they brought him up to Jerusalem to present him to God (as it is written in the law, 'Every male that opens the womb shall be called holy to God') and to offer a sacrifice according to what is said in the law . . . " [Luke 2:22–24].

ANNA: He buys two turtledoves. I'm sure he can't afford a lamb, so he gives the offering of the poor.

SIMEON: Do you think that priest knows whom he is blessing— the hope, consolation and joy of all the earth? (*a brief pause while they watch the ceremony*) They've finished with the ceremony. Come, Anna, we must not miss them. (*calling out loud*) Pardon me, sir, ma'am, would you come here for a moment? (*Joseph, Mary, and the baby are not seen in this play—only in*

Simeon and Anna's response to them. Simeon *and* Anna *communicate to the audience nonverbally that they are coming close.* Simeon *speaks quietly to them, tentatively reaching out to stroke the baby.*) We know! We know who your child is! We have been waiting *so long* for him to arrive! (*shyly, hesitantly*) May I—may I hold the baby?

(*As Simeon takes the baby into his arms and speaks, the* Narrator *begins quietly playing "Of the Father's Love Begotten" and continues until a verse of it is completed.*)

SIMEON: (*taking the baby into his arms*) "'God, (*looking up*)

> now let thou thy servant depart in peace according to thy
>   word;
> for mine eyes have seen thy salvation
> which thou hast prepared in the presence of all
>   peoples,
> a light for revelation to the Gentiles
> and for glory to thy people Israel.'"

NARRATOR: (*still playing*) "And his father and his mother marveled at what was said about him; and Simeon blessed them and said to Mary his mother":

SIMEON:

> "'Behold, this child is set for the fall and rising of many in
>   Israel.
> and for a sign that is spoken against
> (and a sword will pierce through your own soul also),
> that thoughts out of many hearts may be revealed.'" [Luke
> 2:29–35].

NARRATOR: " . . . At that very hour [Anna] gave thanks to God, and spoke of him to all who were looking for the redemption of Israel" (Luke 2:38).

(*As the* Narrator *says this line and sings,* Anna *pantomimes taking the baby and going from person to person, showing them and telling how wonderful this child is.*)

NARRATOR: (*sings*)

> "Of the Father's love begotten,
> Ere the worlds began to be.
> He is Alpha and Omega,
> He the Source, the Ending he,
> Of the things that are, that have been,
> and that future years shall see,
> Evermore and evermore!"

(*The* Narrator *stops playing at this point.*)

ANNA: How I praise God for letting me live to this marvelous day. The child is beautiful, and through him, God will do mighty things! (*She hands him back to Simeon, who makes faces and plays with the baby for a moment and then hands him back to his parents.*)

SIMEON: God is good! I thank God that I could meet you and witness this day of dawning. Great events will surely come through him. Shalom, go in peace. Our great God shelter and protect you!

(*As the Narrator says the next line and sings a verse of a carol,* Simeon *and* Anna *wave as they visualize the holy family traveling away from them down the center aisle.*)

NARRATOR: "And when they had performed everything according to the law of God, they returned into Galilee, to their own city, Nazareth" [Luke 2:39].

(*sings*)

"How silently, how silently the wondrous gift is given.
So God imparts to human hearts the blessings of God's
heaven.
No ear may hear Christ coming, but in this world of sin.
Where meek souls will receive him still, the dear Christ
enters in."

(*After a moment of silence,* Simeon *and* Anna *go to places
where they began the last two scenes. Anna can be down the
steps just part way.*)

NARRATOR: How do you live after a great promise has been kept,
a secret vision seen? Let's look in on Simeon and Anna the
next day.

SIMEON: (*more joyous and vibrant than he has been before*) O
God, the whole earth is full of your glory. I praise you for what
these eyes have seen, this heart has felt. (*interrupts prayer*)
Anna! I didn't see you coming. (*He runs down the stairs and
gives more generous help. As she repeats her "speech," he is
not annoyed but laughs and repeats the second half of each
sentence with her*).

ANNA: (*breathlessly, coming up the steps*) I do not praise God for
the long steep climb up the holy hill, (Simeon *joins in*) but I
praise God for the wonderful view when I arrive. I do not praise
God for the many steps, (Simeon *joins in again*) but I do praise
God that I can still climb them.

SIMEON: I love it when you say that! (Anna *looks a little puzzled*)
Come, sit with me. Take any seat you like, any of them. (Anna
*looks even more puzzled. She playfully starts to take a different
seat, and* Simeon *nods, but she returns to her accustomed
place.*) You look well.

ANNA: So do you. God is good. Wasn't that a gorgeous baby, and his parents! "God chose what is foolish in the world to shame the wise. God chose what is weak in the world to shame the strong" [1 Corinthians 1:27]. (*In this scene,* Anna *the prophetess, sharing insights of other parts of scripture, will be more clearly seen.*)

SIMEON: I'm surprised to see you. I thought it was your day to help with the Sisters of Mercy.

ANNA: I asked Esther to take my place. I wanted to be with you today, especially. Simeon, how did you know?

SIMEON: (*quietly smiling and chuckling at himself*) Anna, I worried too much about how I would know. When the time came, I knew the same way I received the promise. There was a silent voice deep inside. Strange, I wasn't even looking at that moment. I was telling you my story about the storm and the flock, and I felt this inner nudge.

ANNA: (*gently teasing*) It would take quite a nudge to interrupt *that* story. The moment you said it, I knew you were right. My heart said yes also. I will never forget it. (*a comfortable silence*) Then, too, I wanted to be with you because I will miss you. (Simeon *looks up puzzled*) I guess you will be leaving soon.

SIMEON: Me? Leaving??

ANNA: That's what you said, "God, now lettest thy servant depart in peace."

SIMEON: Oh *that.* I didn't mean *today*! I just wasn't ready before we saw the baby, not at all. I'm ready, but there's no rush. I'll go when my days are finished, but I've been thinking— (Simeon *still wants to do a little "bargaining."*)

ANNA: Yes?

97

SIMEON: I wonder if God might let me live long enough to see the child grow and reign over his realm.

ANNA: Simeon!!

SIMEON: Well, maybe long enough to see that beautiful baby become a sturdy youth. (Anna *kindly nods her head "no" and Simeon absorbs this truth.*) I guess my day of departure is probably close at hand.

ANNA: So is mine. For centuries people have longed to see what our eyes have seen. God is good, so when our day comes we may be at peace. Besides, Simeon, since we have seen the dawn, we can at least glimpse a little into the day. I've been thinking about that baby, and I am sure you have, too. When that baby becomes a man, what do you think he will be like?

SIMEON: You are right. Ever since I held that baby, I've been dreaming about that. I don't know all that he'll be, but I think he will take time for old people like us, and babies and young children too.

(*Let this closing section build to a climax, as they develop a shared vision, which comes ever clearer to them and which makes them ever more excited.*)

ANNA: I think he will call men *and* women to be his friends and followers.

SIMEON: (*touching his hip*) He will have a healing touch and care for the sick and suffering.

ANNA: When people are hungry, he will feed them.

SIMEON: I think he will stay simple and unassuming. Some won't recognize him.

ANNA: "He [will] have no form or comeliness that we should look at him, and no beauty that we should desire him" [Isa. 53:2b].

SIMEON: I think he will be able to speak to old farmers and shepherds like me.

ANNA: The common people will hear him gladly. All who hunger and thirst after righteousness will be satisfied.

SIMEON: It will not be easy for him! That inner voice told me that both the child and his mother would suffer much.

ANNA:

> "Surely he [will bear] our griefs and [carry] our sorrows.
> He [will be] wounded for our transgressions . . . bruised for
>   our iniquities.
> . . . upon him [will be] the chastisement that [will make] us
>   whole,
> And with his stripes we [will be] healed" [Isa. 53:5–6].

SIMEON: The suffering and grief will not be the end of his story.

ANNA: His reign will endure forever. (Simeon *and* Anna *stand, eyes fixed on their shared vision.*)

SIMEON: "For unto us a child is born, . . .

ANNA: "Unto us a son is given . . .

SIMEON: "And the government will be upon his shoulder.

ANNA: "And his name shall be called 'Wonderful Counselor,' . . .

SIMEON: "'Mighty God,' . . .

ANNA: " 'Everlasting Parent,' . . .

SIMEON: " 'Bringer of Peace.' "

ANNA: "Of the increase of his government and of peace, there will be no end" [Isa. 9:6–7a]. (*They hold this vision for a moment. Then they turn and walk toward the back and out doors, as the* Narrator *makes closing statement.*)

NARRATOR: Shortly after this, both Simeon and Anna, Jesus' first two disciples, did indeed "depart in peace." People said that to the end, there was in their eyes the light and twinkle of a wonderful secret. "And the child grew and became strong and filled with wisdom; and the favor of God was upon him" (Luke 2:40).

(*From the balcony, the choir will sing "For Unto Us a Child Is Born."*)

✳✳✳✳✳✳✳

SEVEN

Winter Thaw

For Individuals

Imagine. Imagine how people who don't have a living Christian faith feel and live. You may not have to look far to find such folks. They may be your work associates or family members. This dramatic story is about such folks and how one "Messenger" found doors into their lives.

Read. Read about persons in the Christmas narrative who had a hard time believing. Read Matthew 1:18–25 and Luke 1:14–20.

Pray. God, I believe, help my unbelief! (Mark 9:24) Strengthen my faith and my believing. May I know joy and serenity in my believing. And, if I can be your messenger to some searching hurting people, may it be. Through Christ Jesus. Amen.

Then *experience the story.*

For Small Groups, Families, and Classes

Plan a Group Reading of the Script. This drama requires a simple three-person cast. There is no "built-in" narrator, so someone will need to keep the group informed of the setting for the changing scenes.

Discuss the Dramatic Story. Here are some possible discussion questions. Question 1 should be discussed before the play is read; questions 2–5 are for discussion after the reading.

1. In smaller groups of two or three, tell each other about a time in your life, when doubt or questions about your faith were the toughest. If you have moved beyond that time, tell a little about that as well.
2. Do you know folks like Sheila? In what ways are they like her? In what ways are they different?
3. Do you know folks like Ben? In what ways are they like him? In what ways are they different?
4. Have you ever tried to be a Michael? If so, would you tell about that experience?
5. What special opportunities do Christian folks have at Christmas to share a meaningful faith with the Bens and Sheilas of the world? Are there any specific plans you'd like to make?

For Those Presenting the Drama in Public

In addition to the guidance already offered, here is information to aid in staging the drama.

Setting. A present-day community. (It could be yours, if you live in the part of the world that has winter.)

Cast of Characters

BEN: A searcher-skeptic, in his sixties.

SHEILA: A baby boomer in her late thirties, a "spiritual, not religious" type of person.

MICHAEL: A wise, broad-visioned, compassionate angelic visitor. He finds his way to communicate with each person on his or her own wavelength. What shows is not any "angel" manifestation, but the caring, peace, and power for which both Ben and Sheila long.

The Drama

Ben, *heavily bundled, walks from one side to near mid-stage. He is walking in a favorite park. It is clearly a very cold day—winds can be heard. He comes to his favorite park bench, ponders a moment whether to sit, shrugs, brushes the snow off with his gloved hand, and sits down. It is even colder to sit, so he huddles into his coat and pulls up his scarf even higher.*

A moment later, Sheila *comes jogging in from the other side, dressed in cold-weather running clothes. She is kicking her legs high, doing extra exercises to keep warm, hugging herself between arm motions. She is surprised to see anyone else in the park on such a day.*

SHEILA: Hi! (Ben *waves, acknowledging her without speaking. Most of his face is under his scarf.*) Not a great day to sun yourself in the park! (*He puts the scarf down and pulls an ear muff back to hear a little. She continues to jog in place, and repeats.*) Not a great day to spend in the park!

BEN: (*smiles, and with his hand sweeps the rest of the snow off the bench*) Care to share my bench?

SHEILA: (*still jogging in place as she talks to him*) No thanks. What brings you out on a day like this?

BEN: I'm running away.

SHEILA: Running away? From—

BEN: From Christmas! (*expects her to be shocked, is not ready for her response*)

SHEILA: (*rather eagerly*) You too? That's what I'm running from! What bugs you the most?

BEN: Just about everything—the overcrowded malls . . . the over-sentimental church stuff . . . the overheavy social schedule . . . the overempty bank account (*she smiles*)—but I guess, most of all, the hypocrisy of doing all of it. (*She noticeably shivers.*) Hey, there's a nice little place around the corner. Can I buy you a cup of coffee?

SHEILA: Do they have espresso?

(*They walk off, chatting a little above the wind. They come into a restaurant setting, shed layers, and visit more relaxed and amiably. They introduce themselves to each other by name. Michael is their waiter. He takes their order and brings it to them. Then he stands, observing, listening knowingly in the background.*)

BEN: I often come here. It's a quiet little getaway for me. No piped-in "Jingle Bells!" No plastic mistletoe.

SHEILA: The mistletoe is kinda fun! (*They smile or chuckle a bit.*) Have you lived here long?

BEN: All my life. How about you?

SHEILA: I was just transferred here for my job—from southern California.

BEN: The jogging is better there this time of year! (*She nods and they are quiet for a moment.*) I couldn't hear too well in the wind out there. Did you say you were running from Christmas?

SHEILA: Yes, some of it. The only part I like—time with family and old friends—I'll miss this year. I don't have enough vacation time to make the trip. The rest just doesn't mean much to me. I hope that doesn't offend you.

BEN: Not at all. We have that in common. May I ask—how did you come to feel that way?

SHEILA: I guess I've always felt that way. My mom is Jewish, my dad is Protestant—I guess. He never goes to church. As a family, we went to temple or church only rarely. I have a brother, Aaron, and a sister, Ruth, both several years older than I am. Are you sure you want to hear this?

BEN: Oh yes. I love to hear people's stories.

SHEILA: Ruthie was a peacenik and a civil-rights activist. She wanted to volunteer for the Peace Corps, but it just never worked out. Aaron was a super-patriot—until he did his time in Vietnam. He came back disillusioned and fighting a drug problem. There were years those two didn't speak to each other, but we can all be in the same room now. As you might imagine, ideas and opinions flow freely!

BEN: Sounds . . . exciting. And you?

SHEILA: Well, as I said, my family didn't lay any big dogma on me. They gave me freedom to explore. I appreciated that, only—

BEN: Only what?

SHEILA: For all my freedom to search, I never found any religion or cause that excited me. I've tried many different ways—

BEN: Such as?

SHEILA: For a time I did a lot of Zen Buddhist meditation. I still do once in a while.

BEN: Did you ever shave your head and put on a saffron robe and join the, the—

SHEILA: Hare Krishnas? No. I listened, though. It was interesting, but nothing I wanted to get that involved in.

BEN: What else did you try?

SHEILA: You name it: est, holistic health groups, Native American rituals. Have you ever gone to a Native American sweat?

BEN: Can't say that I have.

SHEILA: You should try it—once. You are supposed to come out . . . purified or something. I just came out hot and sweaty. (*smiles at the recollection, pauses*) I even tried to get involved in a Christian church once.

BEN: And—

SHEILA: I left. (*in response to* Ben*'s inquiring look*) The TV preacher who convinced me to try it promised that I would find a lot of love in the church. Instead, I found a rigid way of doing things . . . people pretty tied up with themselves . . . and they weren't all that loving. There was a young man with AIDS who had returned home to his family. Many folks didn't think he belonged at church! I wish the TV preacher had been right— that there is a community that exists to love. I didn't find it and I left.

BEN: I guess all religions have failed you.

SHEILA: Oh, I do have a religion. It's "Sheilaism."

BEN: (*This is one he hasn't heard; he's rather surprised.*) Sheilaism?

SHEILA: Yes, my own private spiritual faith. I believe in God. I must admit I don't know much about God or what God wants. Still, my faith has carried me a long way. It's just my own little voice. It tells me, "Try to love yourself and be gentle with yourself." And I guess it says, "Take care of each other—as best we can." I think God would want us to do that. That's about it as far as my religion goes [see Robert Bellah et al., *Habits of the Heart* (Univ. of California Press, 1985), 221]. You're a good listener! I don't tell many people about this. But enough about me. If I heard you right in the park, you're running from Christmas as well!

BEN: Well, I don't mind a little Christmas, if we could just use moderation. My wife cooks a great Christmas dinner. And it's nice to see the kids and grandkids. I grumble about the gifts—none of us need a thing—but it's fun, especially for the little ones. I guess my problem with the season is me.

SHEILA: What do you mean?

BEN: I don't believe in what we are supposedly celebrating.

SHEILA: You don't believe?

BEN: Not with so much certainty that I want to spend a month celebrating it! I'm sorry, I guess I'm too blunt. You made me feel I could be honest with you. Do I shock you?

SHEILA: (*a bit uncertainly*) I told you how I felt and I want to hear how you feel. Did you always feel this way?

BEN: I've always felt this way a little. It's just gotten worse with the years. I'm afraid I'm something of a skeptic.
    I think it was in college that it really took root. In a religion course of all things! We studied the efforts to prove there is a God. You know—there has to be a source of all things, a cre-

ator of the created. Our belief and longing for God is supposed to be some sort of proof. I was chagrined to discover you can't prove God exists!

SHEILA: I've never thought much about that. Did you quit believing back then?

BEN: No, but I was a lot more humble and uncertain after that. Then I was attracted to people who told me I could know God through prayer, through meditation. One said "practice the presence of God." I read about Desert Fathers and about mystics who said that God was very real to them. I wanted so badly to feel the presence and closeness of God.

SHEILA: And—what did you feel?

BEN: Nothing. I felt foolish. I felt disappointed. (*pauses*) You mentioned before that you practiced Zen meditation. I'd like to hear about that experience sometime. Oh, I realize I'm a very logical, "what you see is what you get" person. I guess that sort of thing just isn't for people like me.

SHEILA: (*Her pager goes off.*) Excuse me, I have to make a call. (*She goes to side of stage and pantomines a phone call. While she is gone,* Michael *comes up and asks if they want anything more and leaves the check.* Sheila *comes back shortly and continues.*) It was work. Something has gone wrong with my program. I'll need to leave soon, but I can stay a little longer. You were telling me that what worked for others didn't work for you.

BEN: Right, and then it got worse. Someone told me, "Look for the presence of God in other people, in relationships, in the church." I looked, all right, and my experience was even more frustrating than yours. One church had a knock-down fight over whether folks could square dance in the church gym! I went to another church, where the family of a pregnant teenager was shunned when they needed the church most. At the next church, a young pastor—who wasn't cutting it, I must admit—was fired without severance pay or anywhere to go. (*bitterly*) There wasn't a next church, not for me. (Sheila *has empathized with his pain throughout. She now struggles to know how to respond.*)

SHEILA: I feel so bad for you. At least I feel a little peace. You don't seem to have any. One frustration after another.

BEN: You've got me started—I may as well tell you, there's more. Just a couple years ago, my devout, loving, clean-living brother died of lung cancer. Never smoked a cigarette in his life! When we knew what he had, we both prayed that he could go quickly and peacefully. But it wasn't that way. I've never seen anyone suffer so. I could barely stand to go to his hospital room. But I couldn't stay away, either. I didn't want to leave him alone. If there is a God, where was God in all that? (*There is a silent, solemn pause.*)

That's why I run away from Christmas! I don't believe in what I'm supposed to believe if this season is to mean anything. (*He tries to lighten up.*) I do have better days, though. I hope to see you again so I can tell you about them. And I know you must go. (*They rise.* Ben *puts some money on the table, then continues, still trying to lighten up.*) What do people like us say when we part? Merry Sheila-mas?

SHEILA: (*smiling*) Keep warm! (*They go their separate ways.*)

(*Music interlude*)

MICHAEL: (*speaks to the audience for a moment as he clears away the cups*) Hello! I'm Michael, a messenger, a mediator, a means of revelation for Mighty God. (*smiles; the repeat of the sound "m" is playful*) For eons I have brought divine perspective to misguided folk. You just saw my present assignment. This time I have quite a problem—two self-contained, opinionated people on my hands. It will take some doing to get through to them.

I'll start with Sheila. (*thinking out loud*) How am I going to get beyond her own little inner voice? (*An idea that pleases comes to him.*) I know! (*pulls out a cellular phone and starts dialing, stands quietly for a moment*)

SHEILA: (*Pantomines coming into her apartment, putting on some makeup, preparing to go to work. She speaks—thoughts, reflections, talking to herself.*) That poor man, so sensitive, so intelligent . . . so sad!

MICHAEL: (*speaking to her through her pager*) Sheila, there's a greater voice than your own little voice! Listen, Sheila, listen. There is so much more than you have yet discovered!

SHEILA: (*puzzled*) I wonder what jerk got my pager number! (*She pantomines getting into her car and driving.*)

MICHAEL: (*dials her pager again*) Sheila, you've tried so many things. But you leave too fast. You don't give it a chance. God's people have more to offer you than you think. (Sheila *is perturbed, looks down at her pager, drives inattentively.* Michael *calls out in alarm.*) Sheila, look out!! (*She makes a sudden turn, veering from a car she would have hit.* Sheila *and* Michael *breathe a sigh of relief in unison.*) Pay attention, young woman, pay attention! (Sheila *looks more shaken but arrives at work and goes to her work station. She turns her computer on and begins typing.*)

MICHAEL: (*dials her pager once more*) Sheila, there's more meaning and purpose than you have yet found. Forgive and be forgiven! (Sheila *takes her pager and with a big gesture turns it off.* Michael *continues.*) That won't turn me off. I have another power source! (Sheila *tries the off switch again, then with great frustration, opens a desk drawer, puts the pager in the drawer, and shuts it.* Michael *continues. He holds a hand over his mouth to sound as though he is speaking from the drawer.*) Sheila, I can't be shut out. Give God's people a chance. You'll find the love you're looking for. (Michael *hangs up. In desperation,* Sheila *takes out the pager and is about to smash it on the desk when she realizes it is silent. She stares at it, shakes it, and nothing happens. She shrugs and puts it back on.*)

MICHAEL: (*to the audience*) I think that was . . . helpful. Now for Ben. (*The next scene takes place in Ben's home.*)

BEN: Natalie! I'm home.

MICHAEL: (*at first from a distance*) She's not here! (Michael *then appears, carrying three books, and* Ben *is visibly shaken.*) She left a note on the kitchen table—Christmas baskets and errands and shopping. She'll be home by six. I hope I didn't startle you.

BEN: Who are you? Are you here to rob me? I don't keep any cash or valuables in the house.

MICHAEL: I'm not here to rob you. I'm here to give you something.

BEN: Give me something? What—

MICHAEL: Something you lost. Your faith. (*Throughout this speech, it gradually dawns on* Ben *what is actually happening.*) I heard what you told that young woman— pretty grim! Actually we've known about your problem for quite some time. Sit down, we need to talk.

BEN: (*with wonder*) If there is a . . . is he (*pointing up*) really upset with me?

111

MICHAEL: Upset? No. Disappointed? Yes. We all are. Mostly for you. You have so many reasons to believe, but you can't seem to get beyond your doubt.

BEN: Is doubt so bad?

MICHAEL: That's a good question, Ben! Doubt bad? As a journey, as a search, no, doubt is very good. But as a way of life, yes, it is bad. That's where you're locked in, Ben. And you're getting older. One of these days we'll be calling you up. In the meantime you are missing so much.

BEN: I know. But I can't seem to shake it.

MICHAEL: Here, let me help you. I took these books off your shelves. (*hands him one*)

BEN: My old philosophy of religion text! This was where I learned how tentative the evidence for God is.

MICHAEL: You didn't read far enough. Remember this? (*flips over a few pages*)

BEN: Pascal's wager! Oh yes, let's see—

MICHAEL: If you bet your life that there is a God and you're wrong, what have you lost? If you bet your life that there is a God and you are right, what have you gained? Ben, you insist on betting on the wrong side! (Ben *wants to discuss this more, but* Michael *moves on, picks up the next book.*) Look at this one.

BEN: What's that?

MICHAEL: Your Bible given to you by your Sunday school when you were in the third grade. (*blows noticeable dust off it*) Read Matthew 1:18.

BEN: (*reads*) "Now the birth of Jesus Christ took place in this way. When his mother Mary had been betrothed to Joseph, before they came together she was found to be with child of the Holy Spirit; and her husband Joseph . . . resolved to divorce her quietly."

MICHAEL: Now read Luke 1:20. The angel Gabriel is speaking to Zechariah.

BEN: (*reads again*) "And behold you will be . . . unable to speak . . . until . . . these things come to pass, because you did not believe my words, which will be fulfilled in their time."

MICHAEL: When Joseph's fiancée became pregnant, he doubted! When the aged Zechariah was told that he and Elizabeth would have a child, he doubted! But both struggled and grew beyond their doubts. They have an honored place in the Bible. I want you to read about one other person, Eleazer Ben Zaddock. Read Matthew 2:4–5.

BEN: (*reads once more*) " . . . and assembling all the chief priests and scribes . . . he inquired . . . where the Christ was to be born. They told him, 'In Bethlehem of Judea; for so it is written by the prophet.'" Wait a minute. There's no Eleazer Ben Zaddock here.

MICHAEL: Exactly. Eleazer was the scribe who found the prophecy where the Promised One would be born. But he doubted that God could act in such an evil time. He doubted that God still cared for God's people. So he gave his report and went back to his routines. He missed the greatest event in history! (*They exchange a look. Ben winces and looks away.*) I have one more.

BEN: (*reaches out to accept the book*) What's this?

MICHAEL: A devotional book from your shelf.

113

BEN: I don't think I have any devotional books.

MICHAEL: Yes you do. Read this. (Ben *starts reading.*) "God does not die on the day we cease to believe in a personal deity . . . " (Michael *picks up and finishes it with Scandinavian accent*) " . . . but we die on the day when our lives cease to be illumined by the steady radiance . . . of a wonder, the source of which is beyond all reason." Dag Hammarskjöld, a wonderful man. Ben, you don't recognize this book do you? (*He shakes his head no.*) It was your brother's last Christmas gift to you.

BEN: (*With more emotion than he has shown, he pushes the book away.*) I've never wanted to handle it. I looked inside and saw how shaky his handwritten greeting was. I couldn't even stand to read it.

MICHAEL: (*firmly*) Read what he said. It was something he wanted you to hear from him. (Michael *opens the book to the front cover and pushes it forcefully back toward him.*) Read this, Ben.

BEN: (*reading inscription*) "To my beloved brother. I enjoyed the journey. Don't let our pain destroy you. Keep the faith. I care." (*puts his head down into his hands*)

MICHAEL: (*stands behind him and speaks gently, backs away, is gone by the time* Ben *looks up*) Ben, give it a chance. Maybe you need to doubt your doubts. Love is all around you. Keep the faith. I also care. (Michael *is gone, and* Ben *looks up, surprised he is gone, knowing something happened, though he is not sure what.*)

(*There is a musical interlude. In this final scene, we are back at the park. It is a warm winter day.* Ben *with coat open wanders around. He carries a trash bag, picking up sticks, branches, and kindling, whistling or humming a bit of a Christmas carol while he does so.* Sheila *comes jogging by. She too is dressed lighter than in the opening scene.*)

SHEILA: Hi! You look industrious!

BEN: Oh hello, Sheila. We have lots of fires when the family comes, so I thought I'd pick up some kindling. The winter storm knocked down enough branches! Sit with me a bit? (*She does so.*) I've been hoping to see you again. I felt bad about our last conversation.

SHEILA: Oh, it was very helpful.

BEN: (*looks surprised*) Helpful? In what—

SHEILA: The truth? (Ben *nods.*) I don't want to hurt your feelings, but I saw where I might be in thirty years, and I didn't like it!

BEN: Ouch! I guess I asked for it. Sheila, some things have changed since I talked to you. (Sheila *murmurs a "You too?"*) I've been thinking. Do you know why we celebrate Christmas when we do? (*She shakes her head no.*) It comes at the winter solstice—the shortest, coldest time of the year. Once Christmas comes, the days grow longer, light and warmth increase day by day. A winter thaw like this is a promise of things to come.

SHEILA: And you've left some of your winter behind. I can sense it in you.

BEN: Sheila, there's something Natalie and I would like to ask you. She loves it when I come sit with her at the service on Christmas Eve, if only to respect and support her faith. The last couple years, I just couldn't go, but I'm going this year.

Then we come home. I start a huge fire in the fireplace and she makes the most wonderful oyster stew. We sit and enjoy it in front of the fire. If there is one time of the year when life seems good and blessed, that's it.

We'd like for you to share our Christmas Eve with us this year. If you don't have other plans, will you come?

SHEILA: (*to herself, recalling Michael's words*) The love I'm looking for. (*pleased and touched*) Yes, I'd love to.

BEN: Say, would you like another cup of espresso?

SHEILA: It's too warm today. I'd love a glass of mineral water, though.

BEN: We have some of that at home. Why don't you come over? You can meet Natalie and we can make plans for Christmas Eve.

SHEILA: Okay, but I want to finish my run. Where do you live?

BEN: Two twenty-two Elm. Three blocks down and turn right. Second house on your right.

SHEILA: (*starts jogging*) Can you keep up with me, Ben?

BEN: I don't know if anyone can keep up with you, Sheila, but I'll try. I'll try. (*He follows her, walking as fast as he can. They pantomine playful conversation until they are out of sight. A musical voice is heard singing the phrase "Good tidings we bring to you and your kin. Good tidings of Christmas, and a happy new year." On the closing note,* Michael *appears out of nowhere, makes a gesture of success and approval, and disappears again.*)